A
LONG DAY'S
DYING

FREDERICK BUECHNER

A
LONG DAY'S
DYING

MERIDIAN FICTION   NEW YORK

FREDERICK BUECHNER

Frederick Buechner was born in New York in 1926. In addition to A LONG DAY'S DYING, *he has published two other novels:* THE SEASONS' DIFFERENCE (1952) *and* THE RETURN OF ANSEL GIBBS (1958).

Meridian Fiction, published by Louis Strick in affiliation with Meridian Books, Inc., March 1960
First printing February 1960

TO

NAYA

with love and wonder

But rise, let us no more contend, nor blame
Each other, blamed enough elsewhere, but strive
In offices of love how we may lighten
Each other's burden in our share of woe;
Since this day's death denounc'd, if aught I see,
Will prove no sudden, but a slow-pac'd evil,
A long day's dying to augment our pain,
And to our seed, (O hapless seed!), deriv'd.

PARADISE LOST
Book X, line 958ff.

A
LONG DAY'S
DYING

C H A P T E R

I

THE MIRROR reflected what seemed at first a priest. A white
robe, which fell from his thick shoulders in crescent folds,
circumscribed with diminishing accuracy the ponderous art
of his great head, and gave to his obesity the suggestion of
vulnerability rather than strength as he sat face to face
with the fact of himself. This effect was intensified by the
resignation with which he suffered what might have been
his acolyte, also dressed in white, either to anoint his
flourishing, gray-brown hair as if in preparation for some
imminent solemnity or to give it a tonsure. The precise
nature of the operation was of apparently little concern to
him, however, for he fixed his eyes simply upon the mirror,
which reflected with similar discrimination not so much
any details of activity as certain implications of priestli-
ness. The activity, the ritual failed to attract his attention
because he regarded instead only the image of himself, of
Tristram Bone, removed from circumstance, with a look of
profound intensity in which there was, nevertheless, no

3

curiosity; a look he had seen occasionally pass between lovers, possible only after a long romance.

The eyes portrayed upon the glass returned his gaze, the eyebrows rose, the mouth drew firm in tacit response, and between the image and its incarnation passed the recognition of the intimacies of a lifetime during the course of which the two had met only occasionally, for the most part at moments of comparative composure such as this, yet knew each other's subtlest transfiguration and most extravagant potentiality. The mirror was only a ruse, the literal translation of an ancient relationship, and in it Bone had seen himself momentarily as a priest. The anticipation of his meeting with Elizabeth quick within him, he found this an observation of considerable poignance and closed his heavy eyes to it.

The interview was further interrupted by the barber, who drew from a cabinet a hot towel that he wrapped about Bone's head and face, leaving a small hole through which he could breathe. For a moment the heat was overwhelming and a shudder just failed to agitate his weight as he absorbed it. Then it subsided and gave way to a great enveloping warmth that dungeoned him in recollections of past and distant heat, of the South, of red clay roads and clear skies. Wandering once down such a road, past the press of pines and mountain laurel, the breathless sweetness of southern odors, grass and red earth still damp from a summer rain, clad in white linen, the perspiration pearled on his forehead, he had been confronted suddenly by a

hound bitch who leaped down a crumbling bank and fell
upon him in an agony of panting heat and rage. His forehead paled and grew cold as he stumbled backwards under
the swift impetus, while swallows, startled from their holes
in the red clay embankment, sprang fountainwise into the
air and circled wildly above a conspiracy of crippled pines.
Clutching his stick, he swung it back and gave the hound a
savage blow on the side of the neck that sent it sprawling
and dazed to the road's edge. In the distance, across an un-
kempt field of cotton, watery blue smoke curled in colossal dalliance.

All this in an instant, followed by the appearance over
the same bank of a tall boy in blue-jeans and a torn shirt
through which his supple body glistened. His thin face
flashed handsomely like a blade in the summer light, and he
shouted something unintelligible and threw himself upon
the dog's assailant. Bone fell heavily to the ground, crushing his hat beneath him, and struggled with the younger
man in the brilliant sunlight. He fought without art against
an adversary who had every advantage but that of weight,
which he, Bone, knew to be his own and tried instinctively
to employ by rolling to the top and pressing the boy to the
red earth that had already dyed them both. He felt the
young body pumping hot against his own, his face thrust
firmly into the boy's tanned neck in a torrid, jig-saw fit of
flesh, and it was for an instant as if they were lovers there.
Then, with a sudden explosion of strength, he managed to
gain the advantage and panted heavily as he kneeled upon

the boy's chest. He was frightened by the red streaks on the face beneath him, but forgot his fear when he saw similar stains on his own hands that clutched the youth's shoulders, on their clothing, and on his hat that lay almost unrecognizable at his side. It was a different red that saturated the head of the hound where it arched back awkwardly into the ditch, whimpering in an extravagance of pain. The noonday sun fell thick upon the pantomime and scorched its silence. Quickly, and as something quite new, he felt the ancient obligation of speech. He knew neither need, desire, nor ability for angry words but spoke with a dispassion that mocked the subdued violence of his position. It had been a mistake. The dog had attacked him, then the boy. He had had no time to explain. He wanted to be on his way. There was no answer, and he thought it safe to arise from his painful crouch. The boy sprang to his feet, went to his dog, and then, looking over his shoulder, asked Bone if he was hurt. Bone replied that he was not, picked up his hat, and continued down the road. The heat was intense and buzzed like many bees. It made him aware of his weariness. The barber removed the towel.

Wizard blood, lured by heat from the enchantment of his bowels and heart to cooler surfaces, flushed the otherwise pale immensity of his face, which was, by the barber's action, revealed to him once more, and with it his former apprehension concerning what lay before him that early spring afternoon to do. That this afternoon in particular was to stand out from among his many similar meetings

with Elizabeth Poor as being somehow of special importance was his idea alone, he knew, and in no plausible way
ascribable to her. Nor could he discover any good reason
even for himself to think it so, unless perhaps his sense that
no human affairs, however amorphous, could endure the
directives of spring without clarifying themselves to some
degree, one way or the other. One way or the other, such
clarification might be his that day, and he welcomed or im-
patiently brushed aside the time that had to pass before
the hour of their meeting came upon him.

As part of that time, prolongation or anodyne, a manicurist approached him now, seated herself on a stool at his
side, and arranged her implements on a small shelf attached to the arm of his chair. He watched her decorously
in the mirror as she took his hand in hers and immersed it
in a shallow tray of tepid, soapy water. It seemed again to
be Brother Tristram, Father Bone, who felt that her fingers
agile upon his and the soft texture of the water were temptation, the reward for temptation overcome, and the forgiveness for temptation unsuccessfully resisted. He heard
her chatter abstracted by the mirror in which he observed
her, learned that he was looking well, that his unusually
long absence from the barber shop had not gone unnoticed,
and wondered that the speaker could sit beside him, his
fingers intimate and safe within her hand as though he had
needed a leader and she now led him, while the voice remained the mirror's. He returned her compliment in general words distilled from the complexities of two months in

the South, among the Blue Ridges, in drawing-rooms
paneled with wormy chestnut, seen through picture windows framed in dogwood, and complicated by voices;
where he had sat with the old lady, Maroo, in a room
whose plaster was tinted with the red clay of familiar
roads, hearing her speak of the history of France as danced
out in Geneva in a spring of her girlhood, of the melancholy French eyes of her father, of her daughter, Elizabeth,
whom he waited now to meet, and of people with whom he
walked through woods and conversed of still other people,
of the old lady herself. Of all this his words to the manicurist conveyed nothing but the fact of his visit and of his
recent return, and yet she replied as if with some understanding of what lay behind them.

An intermission of silence then drew from her histories of
her love, a subject not irrelevant, she knew, sensing in the
unarticulated background of Bone's remarks the presence
of the South, of Maroo, of Elizabeth even. She translated
the varieties of her love into a poverty, first, of generaliza-
tions concerning life as not all peaches, Mr. Bone, of life
comme çi comme ça, the fact that it is, after all, what you
make it and the private property of the woman who knows
and goes after what she wants. Then, with a difficulty implied by her increased concentration over the problem of
his hand and the tiny emory board with which she filed his
nails into nearly perfect pink crescents, she turned to a
more particularized account of an alliance made painful
by the fact that her lover was unable to tell his wife that he

no longer loved her, said just wait, just wait, which, oh, she in turn was unable and unwilling to do. Waiting was cheating and nothing to be desired anyway. What was to be done, all this talking and talking making no difference? It was, for her, hell, and for him, and his wife too. Bone watched and heard all this in the mirror where he also watched himself. The implications there of the priest, which should by themselves have denied him the possibility of participating, himself, in any love like this of hers, were augmented by the more literal reflection of his obesity, which he saw as the more formidable ban of the two. The old recognition of ardors meet enough in other men, but which in a fat man become a profanation, indicated most clearly those ardors with which the manicurist now concerned herself. He grew aware, among other things, of his admiration for her, and of the fact that here was perfection in an audience where his authority at least, seldom questioned at any time, would run no risk of being questioned at all and not simply as a matter of pretty courtesy.

He breathed deeply under the folds of his white robe, thrust forth his free hand, and as if (he tried to convince himself) to Elizabeth, spoke to her of love—that waits and grows, that waits and wanes, that waits but cannot declare itself, that waits and will not be defined. She moved her stool to the other side of his chair and started to work on his other hand while he continued. Love as a flower with petals neither closed nor open but merely ajar, fresh in the memory of having been open, deep in anticipation of closing. Bone's courage met with no impediment; different kinds of love, Greek distinctions, kind and unkind.

It was difficult to remain unmoved by the effectiveness of his own delivery, and he examined his subject with her as he went along, discovering maxims of which he had not been previously aware, deciding that anything anyone cares to say on such a subject, if said with even the least art, becomes a maxim and an authoritative one, so vulnerable are people to the inadequate, misleading words of others.

Who has seen the petals merely ajar, fresh in the memory of having been closed, deep in anticipation of opening, he asked. Not until a thing has passed does one take it, dead, in one's hands, and try to weep life back in it or laugh death deeper there. Let there be no unkindness if possible, let there be no further attempts at making this man tell his wife that he no longer loved her, let there be no sacrifice of the happiness of three for the possible ecstasy of two, let morality dictate as it chose. The barber at the next chair opened a metal cabinet to remove a hot towel, and from it arose thin clouds of steam that misted the mirror and forced their way into Bone's discourse as a kind of incense by virtue of their appearance, as a denial of his seeming priesthood by their contamination of his reflection. He looked closely at his clouded image and saw enough to reinforce the realization of certain of his own inadequacies, of the fact that he was scarcely suited to the entertainments of which he would not allow himself to speak more clearly to this woman, to anyone. He was obliged to shrug his thick shoulders, to laugh even, in refutation of what he had been saying. He dismissed the manicurist lightly as he prepared to depart, not understanding that there might be aversions that she did not share, perversities that he did not guess, that there had perhaps been other fat men.

CHAPTER

II

I N THE lobby of the hotel where he lived when in the city, George Motley awaited the arrival of Tristram Bone and Elizabeth Poor almost completely preoccupied with the skillful reenactment of the classic signs of impatience. He tapped his small foot noiselessly upon the thick carpet, looked at his watch with the intensity of one not nearly so concerned with the hour as with the gesture of concern, and lit a cigarette briskly, blowing the smoke upwards and away with a little accompanying toss of the head in order to retain an unbroken view of the lobby and the entrance through which at any moment his tormentors, his indispensable audience, might come. He accompanied each of these actions with a corresponding facial expression of such delicate accuracy that it was difficult to determine, as his friend Bone had long ago found it to be, whether the total effect was authentic or contrived; whether he did as he did because he had observed the grown-ups doing thus,

12

or because he was himself thus fashioned to do. Though it was not solely in relation to Motley that Bone considered this problem, it was nevertheless in Motley's presence that it most frequently occurred to him.

As soon as he saw them approaching him, down the broad foyer, through groups of people and luggage, Motley put aside all traces of his impatience as unthinkingly and easily as if they had been old toys that he now wished to exchange for new and arose to greet his friends with the curiously shy, tight-lipped grin that seemed always to gild him with a kind of boyishness intensified rather than altogether contradicted by the shrewdness of his small, florid countenance. He was charming as a precocious child is charming who remains clever enough to demand not only the rights to which his precocity, but also those to which his childhood, entitle him. If you do not like me as a child, he seemed to say, you will perhaps like me as an author and scholar, though it is true, of course, that there are some who will not like me at all. These were those who called his charm a cunning disguise and his celebrated novels alone a childishness, and his physical appearance worked equally well for them. In their eyes his boyishness became that of a grotesquely aging boy whose tanned, freckled scalp was as clearly visible beneath the faded red hair that grew sparsely there as were implications of a certain unnaturalness and stealth beneath what they considered to be his unbearably mannered exterior, further clothed on this par-

ticular afternoon by a brown tweed suit and a light over-
coat that he tossed over his arm as he stood up to greet
Elizabeth and Tristram.

"My dear," he said, taking hold of Elizabeth by her
arms and stepping back lightly, cocking his head to one
side and frowning wistfully as if such mature, dark beauty
as hers were not to be viewed too closely, "how good to see
you—Tristram permits it all too rarely. But I forgive him,
and," he released one of Elizabeth's arms and with his free
hand punched Bone lightly in the stomach, "how perfectly
delightful!"

They tried to apologize for being late, but without even
letting them finish Motley protested its unimportance.
"Nonsense," he said, "it has given me time to think—I
have little enough time for *that* usually, what with writing
—and how are Emma and Simon?"

Bone replied that both the German woman who kept his
apartment for him and his monkey were in good health.

"And Lee?" Motley continued.

Elizabeth replied that her son, too, was well and, to all
appearances, enjoying his first year at college.

"Well then . . ." Motley let the next step be theirs.

"How's your new book coming, George?" Elizabeth
smiled at him as he offered his arm and prepared to lead
them out of the hotel to his car.

"Scarcely begun, I'm afraid. Historical, you see, and so
hard to get started. That's why—"

"You're taking us to the Cloisters?" offered Elizabeth.

"To get the last word on the Middle Ages." Bone concluded.

"But exactly! And also," he paused long enough for them to pass through the revolving door onto the street before continuing, "to spend an afternoon with you two clever ones, of course. You should have brought the monkey, Tristram. A monkey in a monastery—only think of it!"

"Monkeys, unlike novelists, George, know when to stop. You don't understand my Simon."

"Ah?"

"And I don't understand your Emma, I'm afraid," interrupted Elizabeth.

"Nor like her either, the good, good Emma."

"That too." She laughed as Motley opened the door to his car for her.

"Such a day!" Motley waved at the blue sky. "Will you be all right back there, old friend?"

"Anywhere," answered Bone. Elizabeth turned over in her mind several times the thought of visiting a monastery.

Because there was scarcely room for him in the front seat with the other two, Tristram sat in the rear, where no shield broke the wind that blew with such force at the speed of Motley's driving once they had left the city proper as to make conversation among them impossible. In the small car with someone as short as Motley driving and Elizabeth sunk way down in her seat so that her hair would be no more blown than was necessary, he seemed to assume a new enormousness. Sitting sideways to give his legs more room, one arm stretched out along the back of the seat, the other upon the door, his head inclined back slightly in order to catch the full glory of the wind, he appeared to be the open car's sole occupant, and the two figures before him no more than instruments on a panel. Swift air rather than earth became his element, and, his eyes closing, his senses knew no other thing. Reality became for him no more than the sting of hair whipped against his forehead, and all else a rushing softness that pressed close about his face like the cushioned palm of a great hand.

The monastery, built in the thirteenth century, had been removed from its native Italy some years before, converted into a museum, and erected upon the long stretch of hills overlooking the river and the parkway that runs beside it on the outskirts of the city. When Motley finally drove up in front of it and stopped, Bone felt his face burn as though he had lain too long in a strong sun. Motley excused himself, saying that there was work he must do and promising that he would rejoin them later. They took their leave of him and proceeded more slowly towards the high stone entrance.

Their encounter with Motley had found and left Bone in good spirits. He offered his arm to Elizabeth, and together they made their way up the worn stone steps. He had become accustomed long ago to the life of organized leisure that admits of a distinction between successful and unsuccessful trips to the barber shop, and his most recent visit there was clearly to be numbered among the former. After a fashion, it seemed to him, he had triumphed—as far as his words to the manicurist were concerned surely, for he had spoken and she had listened with art—but, more importantly, he had triumphed over the mirror and those ancient qualms to which the mirror had given birth, and that triumph was not without its extensions, since it was with Elizabeth that he now walked. She was very beautiful. Each time he made this discovery it was with a new delight, and never more so, he thought, than when he had watched her wave good-bye to George—a quick gesture of her hand, a flash of sunlight in her face and in her dark hair as she raised her head, yet lost, he saw, on the retreating figure of the little novelist.

They walked on silently now, neither of them caring to be the first to articulate their meeting with Motley into an actuality that would have to be further defined then as either a pretty joke or part of a sadness. In the garden about which the cloisters ran, pigeons flickered, and they distracted themselves by merely watching the birds scurry beside them, singly and in pairs, as a kind of escort. Tristram, content himself to say nothing, was nonetheless pleased when Elizabeth, for whom silence was always something of a challenge, suggested an attitude easy for them both by exclaiming on the beauty of the day and, simply, on the *niceness* of having George Motley with them. This made it charmingly unnecessary to carry the matter any further.

"Tristram?"

"Yes."

"Does it really bother you that I don't like your Emma terribly?"

Not the least charming thing about her, Bone thought, was her way of speaking his name in the most serious manner as preliminary to the vaguest kind of question in which she herself seemed to have only a haphazard interest. He smiled as they continued their walk around to the shaded side of the quadrangle.

"You cannot bother me."

They both knew that Emma Plaut, Bone's one servant, did not like Elizabeth, disliked her even as a difficult and important lesson in that grammar of her employer's life to which she ever turned for recreation as well as instruction, but they never spoke of this any more than they spoke of Bone's profound affection for Elizabeth, of which they were also both aware. Bone spoke of it occasionally, but metaphorically. Sometimes Elizabeth understood, or sensed at least that he was speaking on more than one level at once, but her replies were always direct and addressed to the outer portion alone of his meaning. She admired his cleverness. She needed a word for him—nabob, pagoda, these sounded right to her, coursed through her mind as they walked. These came nearer than most to meaning something to her, but what? Fatness, importance, directives, prescriptions on life, a great vulnerability of which, somehow, one did not take advantage? She released his arm as one steps back from a painting. Tristram, she thought, Tristram, wondering if his name were not perhaps the word for which she searched. Possibly his nickname, Whale Bone, the Prince of Whales, more recent of course than Tristram (from his college days she guessed), but one never used these and, if one thought of them, proceeded much as did Elizabeth, who now took his arm again. This was the least one could do.

To be considerate was one thing, to be kind and devoted another, and then to be interesting and colorful and really very clever too was more than one usually went around asking for in a friend. And he was also, of course, rich—not extraordinarily so, one knew, but more than adequately so. He didn't have to worry. One understood. Because Elizabeth enjoyed similar good fortune herself through the generosity of her late husband, the fact of Bone's wealth was a matter of little concern to her in itself, and she was all the better able to evaluate and appreciate its subtler manifestations.

What she considered his monkey's, Simon's, value, for instance, was not lost upon her. She thought of Tristram's life as a rather serious affair, intellectual, stuffy as she was apt to term it, and Simon seemed to her to provide just the correct amount of comic relief. After all, she concluded, a monkey is a ridiculous animal, and how clever of Tristram to recognize the need for just such a ridiculousness among all his literary dinner parties, in his dark, leathery apartment (ruled over by that rather unbearable German woman), and in his life in general for that matter. How clever of him, also, to have taught the little animal so many tricks, though to be sure most of these stemmed from the one trick the monkey was born knowing and didn't have to be taught at all—monkey see, monkey do, you know. Let Tristram gesture with his large hands, and Simon would mirror the gesture with his small ones. It was always like this. Why, Tristram had even bought a small top-hat for his pet in order to have the monkey tip it ever so gracefully to whatever ladies happened to be present at the time. It was wise of Tristram not *always* to take himself seriously.

Tristram knew that his grief at having Elizabeth release his arm as she had done was all out of proportion, and though that knowledge did not become another grief itself, it added to the first which was, however, mercifully brief for in a few moments, long enough for her to recall his nicknames, she had taken his arm again. Again he recognized the extravagance of his emotion—this time of delight—at feeling once more the light weight of her gloved hand upon his sleeve. He wondered then, and it seemed to him that perhaps emotion at a high level escapes definition and that he had been full of the same kind of happiness— he saw the word as a definition and discarded it—the same kind of *ardor* when Elizabeth released his arm as when she took it again. As one temporarily loses the meaning of a word by repeating it to oneself long enough, so Tristram found, for the moment, by thinking of them in this way, that he could not distinguish between happiness and sorrow, and that ardor seemed the only possible word. But this was only for a moment.

Soon he was glad, glad even that he and Elizabeth were not to remain alone together just now, but that there was to be this interval with Motley. There would be time enough that evening at dinner, when there were to be only the two of them, for the clarification he had contemplated that afternoon at the barber's, to which his words with the manicurist had been a kind of prologue. Their promenade came to a halt on the bright side of the quadrangle with the reappearance of Motley.

"Well," said the novelist, "I suppose this is it. They'll call it all wrong again, the critics, and sloppy, but, after all, reality isn't everything. Take those pigeons for instance. Nothing real about them. Completely unconvincing. Nevertheless." He crumpled up a page from his notebook and flipped it into their midst. With a clattering of wings they took refuge upon the roof. "There you are," he said.

"There can't be anything whiter than the white of those birds," said Elizabeth.

"There you are, indeed." Tristram smiled, and in the sun his eyes shone water-clear.

For no apparent reason, the pigeons flew off the roof and settled down on the far side of the garden.

"Don't let me keep either of you from your investigations," continued Elizabeth. "I just want to stand here in

the sun a few minutes." She leaned back against a stone
pillar as she spoke and, closing her eyes, faced the sun.
"It couldn't be more wonderful."

"Back to work then," said Motley, and bounded up a
short flight of worn stone steps and through a door.

"Don't get lost." As she spoke, her eyes still closed, she
stretched out her hand, and Tristram, stepping beside her,
took it softly in his. She opened her eyes and looked at
him, freed her hand and brushed away the hair that still
lay across his forehead where the wind had blown it. Then,
closing her eyes again, she turned towards the sun.

"I'll be along in a minute."

Bone wandered aimlessly down the cloistered walk,
clubbed by the shadow of each pillar as he passed it.

CHAPTER

III

BONE found himself in the chapel. The dark, scarred wood
absorbed what little light strained through the bright
blue, cinnamon, and green stained glass of the lancet window whereon a prophet bore a scroll with *Ecce Virgo*, and a
sun-struck halo birthmarked all who entered there, so that
Bone, still blinded by the spring day without, could see
almost nothing until, gradually, he saw the altar bordered
with lions passant and tongues of fire, the windows themselves, and the choir stall. As he stood there, the dim richness that he had taken at first for silence identified itself
rather as the indistinct benedictions of an organ being
played in some lower portion of the monastery, and the
discovery moved him strangely; for, whenever he found
himself surrounded by the appurtenances of ceremony,
even the earlier ceremony that day of the barber shop, its
mirror and acolyte, his immensity appeared to him to assume a new and peculiar appropriateness that permitted
him to wear it with tremendous dignity as a kind of alb or

vestment. He walked now slowly and with grandeur to the carved wooden image of a saint that stood nearby as though they would exchange some holy confidence, and there he stopped to see with whom it was he shared this sanctuary.

The figure, though something less than life-size, rose higher than he through the half light by virtue of its pedestal. One arm, outstretched as if in blessing, had lost its hand, but the other, folded across its narrow chest, remained intact. The upward stare of the eyes was matched in its lunatic intensity by the lipless mouth opened just wide enough to reveal two rows of tiny, chipped teeth of the same soft red pine as the robe that fell in tight folds about a pair of sandaled feet. Bone reached out and touched them. He touched the spiral curls of hair and beard, the sleeve, the very face itself. The wood was smooth and cool, and he ran his fingers along it until he came to the hand that the figure pressed against its chest. There was a sizeable recess there between the cupped palm and the wooden robe as though the saint might once have held some object, and Bone, though in dread of discovering some decayed remnant of that object or something else of foreign warmth and softness, reached into it. He did this not altogether idly, but as a gesture and with a kind of hope. The recess was empty, nor had the artist made any attempt to represent the folded palm whose outside was so painstakingly carved.

Realizing the inappropriateness of his action, he had

started to withdraw his hand when he discovered that
somehow it was caught there in the saint's. There followed
a moment of panic during which he braced his entire
weight against the pedestal and, pulling as hard as he was
able, tried to free himself, but the figure rocked so dangerously towards him that in even greater fear that it might
fall he ceased his struggling and steadied it as best he could
with his free hand. He looked over his shoulder to see if
anyone had entered. Satisfied that no one had, he turned
again to his task and more delicately this time twisted his
hand first this way and then that until in a moment he was
able to remove it easily. For the first time now he became
aware of the extent of his terror and exertion but, more
strongly, of his maddening embarrassment, the embarrassment of reaching out to pat a dog and having the animal
respond with frenzied, angry barking. He hated the figure
before him and wanted wildly to kick and deface it when,
with a quick flood of self-consciousness and fatigue, he
sank to his knees before it.

He realized that he was acting without thought, and
that one action was leading to another almost independently of the actor, bearing him like an ailing leviathan
to the giddy surface of the sea whence the rush of deep, hidden currents is as obscure as was now to him the low, con-
tinuous music of the mind in unbroken contemplation or
the sound of the organ beneath him where he kneeled. Like
waves his actions in the chapel had folded one into the
other until at last he found himself with aching knees on a

bench that creaked beneath his weight. It was as if he floated, belly upwards and exposed to the cold ocean wind, and if he prayed it was to sink back into submarine safety, the hidden and wise, where he could move once more with fluid speed and ponderous grace.

Towards this end he felt he must speak, explain matters more fully to the saint whom he had seemingly offended, or, more reasonably, to someone who had seen the offense and could understand the precise nature of the tragedy and of his innocence. He felt there should be a reliable witness, impartial as a mirror, to report with overwhelming accuracy each detail not only, as he thought upon it, of his most recent encounter, but of all his experience, of Tristram Bone involved with actuality. A reliable witness, impartial as a mirror but able to retain what it reflected, having seen everything, would somehow absolve him of whatever guilt he might ever incur or have incurred and make of whatever might seem his tragedy merely one of several ways in which things happened. But there was no one. He looked about once more to be certain.

The longer he kneeled there, the more self-conscious he became and consequently the more unwilling to rise, not only because there would be a kind of sacrilege in it, but because he feared the taking of another action that might be thoughtless. On further consideration, however, he decided that he had sunk beneath that rough surface and, rising first to one foot and then to the other, stood up, wrapped his coat about him, and thrust his way out of the dimness of the chapel. When he reached the comparative daylight of the refectory, he mumbled "Amen" in prayer fashion and dabbed away the few small points of blood that sprang from his wrist where he had scraped it.

Elizabeth stood leaning against the pillar with her eyes closed. The heat of the sun seemed a kind of sleep applied from without that lulled her features into repose, and she would have welcomed it with raised palms except that it appeared to forbid all movement. Only the birds, at last, disturbed her. Something alarmed them, they rustled again to the roof, and she opened her eyes. Three or four couples were coming down the far side of the cloisters, and through the gateway she could see more getting out of a bus. Probably the vanguard of a sightseeing tour, she imagined, and went hurriedly up the stairs and through the door by which Motley had left shortly before. After wandering from one room to another, down some more sagging stone stairs and along a row of cells, she reached a small door through which the priests once had passed who conducted mass in the chapel. She had to stoop slightly to get through it, and found herself directly next to the main altar several minutes after Tristram had left by the larger door at the rear of the room. Like him she had to wait for some minutes before her eyes grew accustomed to the dim light, and even then she saw things only gradually. Most difficult of all for her were the choir stalls. From where she stood she was unable to discover exactly what they were and had to stare at them for some time before they identified themselves. Then, to her surprise, they seemed to move, or at least some part of them did, and there was a scurrying noise from their direction. She was not frightened, but stood quite still waiting to see what was to happen. Again there came a scuttling noise, something bobbed up for an instant over the back of the first tier of seats, disappeared and then appeared again. She was certain that it was a head, probably a child's head at that level, and delighted with the thought decided to investigate. At the sound of her footsteps on the stone floor the head appeared again.

"Elizabeth!" it exclaimed.

"Good heavens!" she said. "George! What on earth?"

"Well," his shoulders and chest appeared as he rose to his feet, "did you think you were Bernadette about to see the ghost of Mary Q. Virgin?"

"George," she reproved, "do you want us to be struck by lightning?"

"That's a thought," he continued. "Suppose we get out of here right now." He climbed over the ornately carved front stall and joined Elizabeth.

As they were leaving the chapel she whispered. "Just out of idle curiosity, what were you doing crawling around on your hands and knees in there?"

He stopped walking.

"Really, Elizabeth, I can see you've been drinking again. And after all the promises to Aunt Oyster . . .

after all my entreaties . . ." His voice sounded as if it would break with grief. Then, sharply, "What choir stall? Who was crawling about? Now think! Think! Pull yourself together!" He clutched her by the shoulders. "This is a monastery, you know. Stop that insane laughter. Elizabeth!" He pretended now to be frantic, and his voice grew wilder and more highly pitched. "What will the monks think?" He gestured towards a group of the sightseers who had entered and stood transfixed and through whom he now with mumbled apologies cleared a way for himself and Elizabeth.

It was a matter of some moments after they had found a bench in an empty room before she was able to resume her inquiries. During her laughter Motley, to appear humorously unmoved by his own humor, had assumed a melancholy mien that brightened perceptibly as she continued to speak again.

"George, *please.*"

"All right." He laughed shortly and Elizabeth joined him, politely this time rather than as before. There was a change of mood and of tempo apparent to them both, and Motley saw the necessity of making a more or less serious explanation.

"Well, I was just curious," he said, "in relation to my book, to see if it were possible for a man to hide himself in one of those contraptions."

"Oh, I see," answered Elizabeth, "and is it?"

"Yes, very definitely."

"Well. And how is that going to work into your story?"

"Oh, I'm not sure yet," he said, "I'm not sure yet whether I'll even use it, but when I work on a scene I always like to have all the possibilities at hand. You can never tell when it mightn't come very much in handy to be able to use a choir stall as a trysting place or hiding-hole or more or less anything you can think of, and though it might seem unimportant to some as to whether or not it's actually possible, whether there's really room enough in a choir stall, that's the kind of accuracy I believe in. I mean as long as you can root out a fact like that, why not do it? Because if you're authentic in the details you're somehow or other forgiven for taking liberties in more important matters."

"Really," said Elizabeth. "That's quite fascinating."

"Yes, it is." Motley's interest in the conversation visibly increased. "And in more ways than one."

"Oh?"

In reply Motley smiled his most boyish smile, both shy and challenging, and for the most part successful when, as now, he directed it towards someone of whose affection he was reasonably certain. Only when he was on the defensive did it run any serious risk of failing, and at this particular moment more than ever before he felt in complete control of his position with Elizabeth. In fact it would not be long, he imagined, before he had achieved with her, as with the other attractive women whom he knew successfully, that rather specialized intimacy which is based on a tacit and mutual agreement as to the undesirable grotesqueness of a physical relationship, and since the establishment of such an intimacy held for him something of the excitement of a seduction he was anxious to bring it about without delay. For this reason, although aware of the fact that his loyalty to Tristram as an older, better friend should dissuade him, and although somewhat depressed by this realization, he decided to tell her something of what he had observed earlier in the chapel.

"Yes, indeed," he said, "in more ways than one. I had no sooner ducked down on my hands and knees in that unhappy thing when I heard someone coming into the chapel and realized it was too late to get up and away without being seen and too silly to stay where I was, and so of course I stayed where I was, trying hard to think of something else until I should hear this person leave again. Instead, I heard just about everything else: several small grunts, a scuffling of feet, and then a shaking, knocking sort of noise that was too much for me. At the risk of being exposed as either a lunatic or a peeping-tom I raised my head and took a look. And who, as the saying goes, do you suppose I saw but the dearest of Whales, and what do you suppose he was doing but trying his best and hardest to get his hand back from a wooden saint in whom he had somehow or other managed to get it stuck!"

Motley paused to italicize the climax of his narrative and to see what Elizabeth would say. He was not sure what reaction to hope for from her just as he was not sure as to the nature of the story he was in the process of telling. This worried him briefly.

"He looked for all the world," Motley continued experimentally, "like a small boy who got his hand stuck in a cookie jar and was willing to do anything short of cutting it off at the wrist in order to avoid being caught by someone. Yet at the same time I couldn't help thinking that if the young Whale had been discovered in such a position by his mother all she would have done undoubtedly would have been to cajole it off again and tell him how happy it made her to see her little Tristram eating."

"Whatever did you do?" asked Elizabeth.

"Why nothing, as a matter of fact. For some reason or other I didn't think I should let him know I was there." Motley spoke these last words with a new conviction as to the nature of his tale and slowly as if to show a transition from the laughable. It was with this part of the story, this particular confidence, that he hoped to be able to purchase the intimacy he sought.

"*I felt as though I were seeing something that I shouldn't be seeing at all. . . .*"

He knew exactly what he was trying to do now and also, as exactly as possible, the kind of response he hoped for from Elizabeth. As soon as she spoke he knew that he had failed.

"Yes." She said this without emphasis, yet in such a way as to denote complete agreement with the self-criticism he had implied only so that she might sympathetically deny it.

"What did he do then?" she continued.

"He got his hand free," Motley answered. "And then," he paused, "then he left."

"Are you joking?"

"No," he said.

Elizabeth was actually no more certain than Motley concerning the nature of his story, but she was unwilling to question it further. Her reticence was almost virginal, as though she were confronted with a potential seducer, and there was in it a similar amount of curiosity. Nevertheless, she said nothing.

The room in which they stood was bare except for a long table with benches on either side of it, and the daylight was sunless and gray there. Elizabeth saw it as coolly barren and harsh as a headache and wished herself away. With Tristram, she thought, rooms did not become like this. There was a richness of texture about him that forbade it, and they seemed to her to assume, when he entered them, a quilted, padded quality rather like an elaborate bassinet. She wondered vaguely if such had been the state of the chapel during his struggles there, and was almost on the point of absently asking Motley, who had of course been there too, when she realized with something of a start that she had perhaps offended him, or he her. In either case, it seemed to her, she should try to appear as if the fault had been his, and this could be best done by maintaining a silence through which she might seem neither merely pensive nor really angry but something in between, hurt perhaps. She glanced in his direction and saw him in profile bending down to observe the Latin motto carved at length about the edge of the table. It was as wrong for him, she thought, to have seen Tristram in the chapel as it was for him to have told her of it. But it was a rather amusing story. She wondered now why she had not been more amused. And he looked so little there bending over the table, like a puppy that knows it has offended and goes away wistfully until recalled. She felt that her relationships, when colored by Tristram, became somehow complex, involved and, at last, difficult for her to understand or manipulate very successfully. It was bad enough to have it the case with Tristram himself, but now it was happening again with George. She deplored this and resolved to speak to him simply, as though nothing had happened at all. Nor has it, she thought. Motley, however, spoke first.

"How about going down to see Lee tomorrow?" he said. At the sound of her son's name she raised her eyebrows in surprise.

"Whatever made you think of that?"

"Well," he answered, "I'm scheduled to give a lecture there tomorrow evening and it just occurred to me how nice it would be if we could go together. I'd forgotten he was there. It's not far, you know." He named the university where Leander Poor was nearing the end of his freshman year, and the number of miles that separated it from the city.

"Oh I know that," she said. "His father went there you know."

"Oh, of course," answered Motley.

"That might just be very nice," she mused. "It might just. Let me see . . ."

Motley maintained a vacant, noncommittal expression that would scarcely have deceived any observer more attentive than Elizabeth into imagining that it made no great difference to him whether or not she consented to accept his suggestion. Clearly enough, the difference it made was vast. He ran his fingers along the edge of the table. What had seemed his defeat, her unsuccessful reaction to his account of Bone in the chapel, could be altered completely now by her consent. He wanted to rush over and shake her by the shoulders until she answered affirmatively.

"Yes," she said, "yes, that would be lovely. I can do it. When would you like to leave?"

"Well, I must be there for a luncheon engagement at one."

"Oh but I never get up much before noon or a little before, and that wouldn't give me time . . ."

The main victory his, Motley could afford to make these minor concessions. "Then why don't we simply plan to meet after the lecture and I can take an earlier train?"

"That's fine," she replied. "I'll telegraph Lee right away that I'm coming. He's wanted me to for some time now. Where do you suppose Tristram is?"

"Wouldn't want to guess," said Motley. "I'll see if I can find him." As he disappeared through the door Elizabeth went over to one of the benches, sat down, and tried to phrase a telegram in her mind.

C H A P T E R

IV

THE EXTENT of Bone's monkey's knowledge or, more exactly, of his ability to retain or to assimilate what he saw, was a matter for much conjecture and a question often considered but seldom expressed as if from a fear that, once asked, it might be answered. The animal was ubiquitous within the bounds of his master's apartment and could creep either silently or with considerable commotion from one room to the other just as he could, upon his arrival, either crouch unnoticed in a corner or gibber and scratch in full view of whatever company happened to be present. At the same time, it was impossible to deduce any set formula for the occurrence of these two phenomena as is possible, with a dog for instance, to know with some degree of certitude when and with whom it will bark, and when and with whom be silent. It was only the geography and not the metaphysics of the monkey's actions that admitted of prediction; for with some regularity, when conducting one of his subtler and more silent vigils, he would choose as his post a tiny painted chair, left over from the impossibility of Bone's childhood, that stood away from the windows on the dark side of the heavy mahogany writing table and gave its occupant an unbroken view of all that happened in the room. This little chair might well have been especially fashioned for him. Its rush bottom was far more readily conceived as having been built for his small posterior than for any version, however reduced, of his master's, and the pattern of dark rosebuds on a purple background seemed less contrived for a nursery than for blending with the dark brown of his small person, thereby assisting him in his espionage, curiosity, simply his desire to remain quiet and unbothered, or whatever. When he chose to join in and display himself, however, the predictions grew of necessity vaguer, for then he might occupy the arm of a chair, the top of a bookshelf, the heavy writing table or, for that matter, any elevated, conspicuous position, and the only person who claimed a more detailed insight than this was Emma Plaut, Bone's one servant; but she tended to despise the monkey and was paid little heed in any matter concerning him. Emma Plaut also had an answer to the basic question as to how much the monkey knew, and her answer was that he knew everything.

It was because she thought the monkey, whose name was Simon, knew everything that went on in the apartment (she, Emma, did not) that she for the most part so heartily disliked him. It was annoying to her in the extreme that Simon was permitted at interviews of which her only knowledge had to be derived from whatever loud words they might occasion and which she could hear from the kitchen or, when she had an excuse for being there, from the library adjoining the living-room. She was a servant in the old manner, the manner of the Germany she had left when still a girl something more than thirty years before, and her primary concern was consequently with keeping her employer's affairs in order, and her chief recreation in storing up, for no specific purpose, treacherous or otherwise, all that she could glean of his comings and goings, his plans for the future, and his past. She had indeed a curious perception in these matters and made good use of whatever opportunities for learning more might come her way. But so many more came Simon's. This was their unresolved quarrel and also the strongest bond between them. When she was not busy hating the monkey, cursing him in overheated German, she came near to being very fond of him as of an accomplice rather than a rival, and would scratch his shoulders for as much as a half an hour at a time in the kitchen, or even take him to the park with her on her day out. These intermittent kindnesses she kept as secret as possible. It seemed somehow wise to let them think she really disliked him, and, as a matter of fact, for the most part, she did.

As for Tristram Bone, neither affection nor dislike entered for her there so much as an overwhelming dependence. Naturally, she kept her distance, told him directly nothing of her restricted activities away from his apartment, and asked directly nothing of this nature from him. Her method was far more conspiratorial. To draw him out on the subject of himself she had countless devices—ways of appearing at times when she knew him in need of a companion: in the morning when he had finished his coffee or in the late evening when, she discovered, a glass of milk and a liverwurst sandwich, or merely the offer of either, would work wonders; and there were more subtle ways than these: implications by the sound of her voice, the way she held her flannel dustcloth, or unusual receptivity; methods of giving him telephone messages in such a way as to make further explanation from him almost obligatory—many such tricks which she never went so far as to enumerate in her mind, but which she knew, and the particular value of each, as well as she knew her catechism or the way to make herring salad on New Year's Day. In much the same manner she was able to register bits of herself with him, but this was not nearly so important because she could always go to see her uncle, who ran a small delicatessen in the city and was almost as dependent upon her in this way as she was upon Bone.

Thus did Emma Plaut spend her life, and ten years of it had already gone by in Bone's service. Few crises arose to disturb her. One, shortly after coming to work for him, was the arrival of Simon. The shock was substantial. Some friends had brought him as a joke, and when Bone decided to keep him she even went so far as to consider a swift departure. But then there was something about the monkey's face that won her. Somehow it reminded her of home, of younger days. Indeed, though she was entirely unaware of it, if one had set upon the monkey's small head a wig of gray hair parted in the middle and drawn back into a tight bun, dressed him in the proper clothing, and then transformed Emma Plaut into the little girl she once had been, she, Emma, would have flung herself into the animal's arms and asked for a fairy tale or permission to go watch the rich ladies and gentlemen drink the bitter and celebrated waters of the small town where she and her grandmother lived. In this way, Emma accepted Simon; but this was of course before she learned that it was possible at times to hate him. That possibility was never richer than the evening of the day of Bone's trip with Elizabeth to the Cloisters. Because her employer had taken his companion elsewhere to dine, she was left alone with the little animal.

Simon had left his small chair by the writing table and was crouched on the arm of a large leather one, his thin shoulders hunched together, shivering slightly. All the lamps were extinguished but one that stood nearby, and his monkey glance was fastened intently on the portion of bare floor on which the light shone. Someone had dropped a cracker there, and around it, in curious patterns, as though engrossed in some complicated game, scuttled a cockroach. It was difficult to know whether Simon's stare was one of sympathy and understanding of the familiar game of eating, or one of fright and horror at the half-remembered and partially understood, or simply of wanton curiosity, but it

was evident that no movement escaped him. The insect
now limped, its rear portion dragging along the floor with
flimsy, useless legs sprawled out, feelers ticking left and
right in parody of an ancient grope, now crawled swift and
smooth, all black legs primed and feelers sweeping, fluctu-
ating with art and assurance. The monkey glanced neither
to the side nor to the rear as if from the hope that had become a conviction that so rare a moment as this must
surely preclude the necessity for vigilance, and consequently failed to notice Emma's entrance.

She entered quietly and stood by the door watching. The
monkey flattened himself upon the chair and reached out
his long arm towards the floor. As the insect approached
the crumbs, Simon flicked it away with a hairy finger. It
fell on its back, righted itself with a frenzy of swarming
legs, and crawled once more towards the cracker. Again the
monkey flipped it back, and again the cockroach speeded
in the same direction. This time Simon picked it up in his
hand and held it to the light where he could better examine
it. It struggled in the dark well of his fingers and finally
managed, by skillful use of feelers and legs, to crawl half of
the way out before the other hand drew near and pressed it
back again. When it reappeared it was with broken feelers
and more swiftly whirring legs. More gently this time
Simon thrust it back, but at the same time tightened his
grip. Then, slowly, he opened his hand to reveal upon his
palm the half-crushed insect, the black mystery of its
underportions exposed to the light, its multitude of legs

vibrating faintly. Simon withdrew his glance and looked around his shoulder as if from behind a rock. His moist, introspective eyes gave no evidence of seeing Emma by the door, nor did they look exclusively in that direction, but once around the room, a bland stare, and then back to his hand. His lipless mouth widened to show his teeth, and he bounced lightly up and down on the chair, clenching his fist so that nothing could fall from it. When he was still again, he lifted the cockroach up and bit it experimentally, held it close to the light, and then bit it again.

"Ach, filthy!" shouted Emma, who left her position by the door and came rushing towards the monkey. Before she was able to reach him, Simon leaped from the chair, scampered across the carpet, and sprang to the writing table, scattering a folder of letters that lay there.

"Off! Off!" cried Emma and continued the chase, but again Simon escaped her, this time to one of two tall silver candlesticks that stood shoulder high on either side of the fireplace, thence to a low table by the couch and finally, with much scrambling, to the top of the half-open door where he huddled in a moment of repose. Emma saw her advantage and taking the door in both hands gave it a great swing outwards that hurtled the monkey across the room. He hit the wall and fell to the floor with a kind of squeaking lament, picked himself up and ran into the darkness of the hall. Emma followed him, switching on the lights, but was unable to discover him anywhere. Her thin face was flushed from the exertion, and she panted heavily

as she continued to look about the hall. She even switched
the lights off again, hoping to catch sight of the monkey's
shining eyes, but still saw nothing and finally, with a grunt,
collapsed into a chair. She sat there silently for some time
and then cursed into the darkness with more resignation
than wrath.

It was later that night, considerably later, and long after
Emma had turned to sleep and Simon to whatever wounds
he sustained, that Bone and Elizabeth Poor returned alone
and entered the living-room whence all signs of the earlier
conflict had been removed except for the letters, which still
lay on the floor where they had fallen. Bone noticed them
there, picked them up slowly and examined each one before
replacing it on the table much as in the theater the curtain
will rise upon a servant who, by tidying up the implausible
three-sided room, lends to it a greater reality, strangely
soothes the audience by giving them time perhaps to recollect the part that they must play, and prepares the player
himself for the first great shock of playing. Bone's figure
bending painfully in his labor, the sight of his heavy face
lit from beneath by the lamp on the table when he stood
up, scarcely added to any sense of reality, and it was difficult to imagine Elizabeth Poor as needing time to recollect
the part she was to play, but it gave Bone opportunity to
prepare himself, to realize that his was no minor rôle but
one of importance and responsibility. He put the last letter
in the folder and then sat down next to Elizabeth, placing

it upon the table between them. He reached into the pocket of his coat, found nothing there of whose presence he was not already aware, and drew nothing out of it.

"Oh Tristram," he said.

"Oh Tristram," she repeated.

"In the palace there lived a king," he continued, "of great power and influence. Do you know the story?"

"I don't know," answered Elizabeth. "Who was the king?"

"A very unusual woman."

"Not a queen?"

"No. A king."

"All right then. I don't know the story."

"In that case I shall continue. This case, I beg your pardon, this *king* had two suitors, and the suitors were sisters actually though they only suspected each other's existence and had never met. In fact the king knew only one of them himself (or herself). No one was quite sure. The king also had a son who was, after a fashion, also the son of one of the suitors. Do you follow?"

"No," said Elizabeth. "Is that your handwriting?" She indicated a letter without an envelope that protruded from the folder he had placed on the table. He leaned nearer the light.

"Yes, it is. You can see it is."

"May I read it?"

"No," he said. She picked out the letter.

"I shall go on with the story," and so he did, as if he did

not know it well himself. It became very sad and very complicated and scarcely a story at all, for nothing happened of any consequence. The other suitor whom the king either knew or did not know, whose existence the first suitor only suspected, became more important as he grew more vague. Bone spoke of him as a secret, and as if the secret were that there was another secret which concerned yet another and so on, and so forth, like mirrors reflecting each other into obscure infinity. Only the king, through a variety of metaphor, emerged as an actuality.

"She was," he said, "a wall against which, or against whom, others knocked their heads, not in anticipation of the pleasure that would result when the knocking had ceased, mind you, but because of the glory of the . . ."

Elizabeth held the letter near the lamp and started to read from it. "Gentlemen," she pronounced, "I am enclosing herewith a check for such use as was agreed upon when last we met. You will discover . . ."

"Elizabeth, it was the wine," he said. "The wine we had with dinner, the wine we had before dinner, the wine we had after dinner, that makes me have to tell you a story now. It was also the manicurist this morning I think. And that indescribable monastery, where . . ."

"You will discover," continued Elizabeth, "that I have sent something more than the sum originally proposed, and I shall leave the disposition of the balance entirely within your hands with the one stipulation that you do not . . ."

"This manicurist. I was moved to advise her on an affair of the heart." He laughed.

Elizabeth flicked the letter to bring it straight again, making a cracking noise, and read on. "One stipulation, that you do not use it towards the erection of bars, alarms, or barriers of any kind whatever. If you will permit me a single ostentation," she lowered her voice to a curiously accurate approximation of Bone's, "let me say that I am unwilling to have my name associated with any organization of this sort that does not concern itself primarily with the demands of freedom," she paused, "and kindness."

"There are those," he said, "there are perhaps three or four," he said, "who would question my authority in affairs of that sort, but in some manner I am qualified. I think that it is possible to gather instruction as you go from matters of an entirely different nature, to understand some part at least of love though you have never . . ."

"Our friends are not so bold but that they must be encouraged to come to us." She glanced over at his face, only half concealed from her by the lamp between them. It looked like a Roman bust of the decadence of that empire, ponderous, sightless with eyes closed, and placid as a cloud or an entire bank of cushioned clouds on a day without wind. His loose, uncombed hair, thin and receding at the forehead, grew in profusion about his ears and might have been the tapering of a wreath or a dark break in clouds. She twisted about in her chair so as to face him, and was about to start reading again when he interrupted her by raising his soft fist and letting it drop to the arm of his large leather chair.

"Once when I was in the South," he said, "not this last time but way before that, before Maroo had come to live on your property down there in Carolina next to mine even, I went to an aquarium, and I remember that I came across one particular small tank in which there had been put a whole regiment of tropical fish. They were all darting in and around the coral formations and those extraordinary anemones and the like except for one that more or less lurked in a sort of small cave in the coral. He looked as though he might have been the only representative of his species in the tank, at least I couldn't see any others like him, and he simply stayed there in his cave waving his strange, filmy, veil-like fins. I watched this for some time when all of a sudden the whole tank, as though at some noiseless signal, swam towards that lone fish and started to mob it, to mouth it, to death. It was a slow process though the victim seemed to struggle only halfheartedly, but they worked their stupid, rubbery mouths so wildly that at last they managed to sever its head from its body. The body they let twitch off unnoticed, but they pressed close about the head whose mouth continued to open and shut and whose eyes still stared ahead, living still, yet as though they were unaware that they no longer served a body, were no longer part of a life." Bone let his hand fall off the arm of the chair so that his fingers touched the floor, and opened his eyes. "Soon, mercifully, I became aware of the pane of glass that kept us safe from one another, and then I leaned my head against it. It was very cool."

Elizabeth continued to look at him—a priest he seemed for a moment, or a saint. She remembered Motley's story of the chapel, realized vaguely that she could think of no fat saints, unless Aquinas, perhaps Aquinas, no other. She returned to the letter not, at first, to read it, but merely so as not to stare at Bone, and then, as she looked further, to read it: "Nor can we so boast of their affections as to think they would willingly stay with us without our small solicitudes during their stay; but we can say, and I, for my part, do say, that they must in no way be forcibly detained, nor may we by any device prevent them from taking their leave whenever they should so desire it."

"You may laugh," he said, "if you like, but I can soothsay from such scenes, and from them I can understand some part of love though I have never . . . dear, good Elizabeth, are you listening at all?"

Elizabeth left her chair and walked to the window where by the moon's light she was able to read the concluding paragraphs of the letter: "I shall hope to hear from you on whatever action you may take in this matter, and shall endeavor to make you a visit as soon as I am able to do so." She returned now to her own voice. "In the meantime you have, as ever, my best wishes. Sincerely, *Tristram Bone*." She almost shouted his name, raising her voice as she pronounced it so that it seemed a command or a salutation, and remained by the window during the complicated silence that followed. It was he, at last, who broke it.

"I told you not to read it," he said.

"Well, it doesn't make much difference," she replied, "I've no idea what it's all about anyway. A booby hatch?" Bone turned his head towards her and smiled broadly.

"Here's your hatch," he said. "Where's your hurry?" He rose from his chair still smiling. "I'm always frank at the wrong time. It's the wine. Don't go really. It was such a day." Elizabeth crossed to the door and stood for a moment on the threshold. Bone followed her as far as the corner by the writing table, where he drew out the tiny purple chair with the dark red rosebuds on it and placed it on the part of the carpet where the moon shone like spotlight. With some effort he lowered himself onto the floor beside it. She looked extraordinarily young in the doorway, even more so as she laughed, he thought.

"Good night," she said. "I'm off to see Lee in the morning you know. See you soon."

"Have a good time," said Bone, "and tell me all about George's lecture."

"I will," she said. "Be good."

"Good night," he answered in a voice scarcely more than a whisper, and as she disappeared into the dark hall he raised his hand near to his face and waved his fingers sleepily, still sitting on the floor by the little chair. He heard her heels click on the floor in the hall, then stop suddenly.

"Scat!" she cried. "Scat, scat, scat!" He heard the door open and shut behind her.

"Good night," he said once more. Uncomfortable as his position must have been, it was not long before he fell asleep, the one lamp still burning between the chairs they had occupied. A light wind started outside and came through the open windows in short gusts, rattling the venetian blinds. The noise worked itself slowly into his dreams and became a great bird's wing there until, as the wind grew gentler, passing silently through the blinds and only rustling the curtains, it became instead the puzzled whisper of a girl.

CHAPTER

V

ELIZABETH was awakened the next morning by the sound of children's voices beneath her bedroom window. She tried first to ignore them, or to hear them as a rhythm only, and thus to incorporate them into the sleep that she wished to reenter, but in spite of herself, though her bedroom was on the second floor of her small gray house squeezed between two large apartment buildings, she heard the words themselves and was obliged to listen.

"Shut up!" said one.

"Shut up yourself," said another.

"Oh go and kiss a colored cook." There was a scampering noise on the pavement and the sound of something being dragged along without wheels.

"Stop it, stop it, stop it. You stop it now or else!" A deeper voice joined in that Elizabeth could not decipher, and then a silence. She considered getting up, but discarded the notion in favor of the cool side of her pillow, to which she turned, closing her eyes and caressing her bare shoulder with her cheek. She realized, vaguely, half asleep, the antiquity of the situation, located herself by it as it is necessary to locate oneself with each awakening, and drew a kind of comfort or reassurance from seeing herself a woman awakened by children, part of an old joke. She smiled and loved herself for smiling, felt her shoulder soft and warm against her cheek. From the street there came more noise, only one child now, the monotonous, ancestral song of children, sing-song, wordless, without emotion, a kind of lullaby. With her eyes closed she forced a vision of the singer—a little girl, it appeared, crouched on the sidewalk beneath the awning that stretched from the door of the building to the street, playing with something. The doorman kept bending over and patting her on her backside, but she paid no attention and continued to sing. It was a clear, sunny day, more of summer than of spring. Elizabeth wondered at the accuracy of her conscious dream and thought of going to the window and looking out when there was a knock at her bedroom door. The little girl ran away as she opened her eyes.

"Come in?"

A colored maid entered and with her the smell of coffee.

"It's just noon, Mrs. Poor. Shall I bring your breakfast?" Elizabeth looked at her clock and nodded. The maid departed, and she sat up in bed, leaned back again upon her pillows, and stretched out her arms as if in supplication. Glancing to the window she saw that the day was bright as she had dreamed or as she had seen, it was difficult to know which, and noticed that the child had stopped singing. The only sound now was that of the traffic passing by, the anticipatory noise of gears being shifted from one level of effort to another, an occasional horn. She tried to remember at what time she had gone to bed and then counted up the number of hours she had slept. It was sufficient, more than sufficient, and she was relieved; she had imagined it less. The day ahead of her seemed immediately easier, for she thought of sleep as the ascent of a bird or a flyer—the higher you climbed the more effortless the journey down, gliding, wings caught up on the wind sometimes and carried along by it, or merely outstretched to give direction to the inevitability of descent, to guide easily a slow and undemanding progression. As a girl she had thought of it that way, and before that as a child. She thought of Leander, her son, and realized that this was the first time she really looked forward to her imminent visit to him.

She had not seen him for several months, and though this fact had not heretofore troubled her or him either, if his occasional letters were just evidence, she nevertheless discovered in herself now what she was pleased to imagine a long-standing desire to perform this possibly neglected division of her maternal duty. Thus having found more of a purpose than simply to please herself and, incidentally, Motley, she looked forward with increased enthusiasm to the trip and, as a matter of fact, to more even than that. She had been there often before with the first Leander, Lee

Poor, her husband, who had died while their son was still a small boy, and she was happy always to renew the lingering romance she permitted herself with the recollections of her girlhood. The maid returned with her breakfast tray.

By one she was dressed and ready to depart. Calling her maid to her in the living-room, she directed her to tell anyone who might call that she would return Sunday and would be in all Monday morning. She was about to add to this a special message for Tristram Bone when she remembered that she had told him of her trip anyway, and decided against it. She looked slowly once more about the room, marking in her memory the position, color, and shape of every piece of furniture there, imagining consciously and as part of a game, aware of its falseness, that she might never see any of it again or, if she did, that it would be somehow altered, never quite the same. A few moments later she was in her car and on her way; beside her, on the seat, her broad-brimmed hat and, next to it, a copy of Motley's last novel, *Daylight's Dauphin*, which she was taking to Leander.

Before her stretched the West Side Drive, and to her right the river lined with docks and the prows of liners. Her memory pleasantly titillated, she wondered at the recurrence that day of a nostalgia connected with a particular portion of her youth, and only gradually realized that it was no coincidence but the logical outcome of following, for the first time in some years, an old path, a series of old paths. She could even predict, once this discovery was made, what would touch her next and speeded up to hasten it, but the predictions were largely wrong, or at least inadequate, for it was the unanticipated that most affected her. Once she was out of the city, when the highway turned through open country, the tricks of sun on groups of trees, the shapes of green, and the mixed fragrance the wind carried in through the car windows, became more important than any building, sign, or flight of road that she was able more definitely to recall, and at last these also faded, and she grew intent only upon her journey as a journey and upon the mechanics of her arrival.

After some time the monotony of the wide, straight highway and the cessation of her thought were broken by a traffic circle at which she turned off down a smaller road that led down a hill, across a bridge, and then up another hill to the college town a few miles away. As she crossed the bridge a break in the trees revealed a glimpse of pseudo-gothic towers flat against the bright sky, and in a few moments she drew her car up at the entrance of the inn where she was to spend the night. She had not expected Leander to meet her there, but when, in actuality, he did not, she felt herself somehow slighted or at least misunderstood, as if her son should have been able to sense, in spite of their agreement not to meet until later, the need she would have acquired by virtue of her drive for the sight of a familiar face in the midst of this most familiar town. She enjoyed the gentle sadness occasioned in her by this neglect and contemplated with correspondingly greater poignance her return, the return almost of an exile, she thought, and years later at that, to the scene of earlier gaiety. Whatever else had changed since then, she had not, and there was a kind of excitement for her in that realization. She did not change. This was sad, but it was also not sad. It was a curious smile she gave to the desk clerk who suggested to her that the terrace behind the inn was ideal for cocktails at this time of day and of year and agreed to tell her son, when he came, that she would join him there.

The window of her room looked down upon the terrace in question, littered with round green tables each pierced by a vivid umbrella and already more than half filled with people, young for the most part, undergraduates in gray flannel and seersucker and their young ladies with hair shiny from much brushing and clad in dresses cooler than the season seemed to require. Beyond the terrace stretched the implausible green of a golf course; and, where a rise in the ground broke all further view but that of the sky, rose a tall, square tower gilded, like the rest of the scene, with the exaggerated light of late afternoon. From the height of her window, no single voice was distinguishable to Elizabeth Poor, but instead, and together, they made a pleasant melody, singsong and apparently wordless, to which she listened for a few minutes, her hands light on the sill, before resting.

The sun was lower but still bright when, a short time later, she descended to meet her son. The complex richness of color and sound confused her momentarily as she stood uncertainly, shading her eyes as she looked to find him among all the others there. When, at last, she did, it was so abruptly and with such speed that she saw him for an extraordinary instant not as her son but as simply another young man on whom her glance had chanced to fall. He stood in profile, his blond hair damp as if from recent combing, his hands in his pockets. He had taken her by surprise, she saw him for a moment through no mother's eyes, and yet the rarity of the instant supplied her with no revelation as far as either he or herself was concerned. In another moment the recognition was completed as she kissed him on his tanned cheek and asked him, with an enthusiasm that betrayed some lack of curiosity, how he was. The conversation at the green tables had reached such a pitch by this time that she could not hear his reply and was only partially aware that he was introducing her to another young man who had accompanied him. Without trying to say anything more above the noise, she allowed herself to be led to a table on the grass and only when she was seated there realized that the other young man was still with them.

"I'm sorry, but I don't believe I heard your name," she said, and he replied that it was no wonder, and that his name was Paul Steitler. She guessed him older than her son, as near to thirty as Leander to twenty, and wondered if it could be possible that they were classmates. They talked, and she learned that, no, he was in fact an instructor in the English Department, and that he was to accompany them to Motley's lecture that evening.

"It's Mendelssohn," he said, "without any doubt at all."

"What's Mendelssohn, Mr. Steitler?" She was asked to call him Paul.

"Their talk, I guess. This is one of the great sights, Mrs. Poor, and one of the great melodies. Just listen to them all without listening to any one of them." With a wave of his hand he indicated all of the tables. "Where else can you find such happiness?" He smiled at her.

"Yes," she replied, returning his smile, "but it's noisy too."

"But you'll forgive them that, I hope?"

"I suppose," said Elizabeth.

"Yes," he continued, "because I'm the only unforgivable one myself."

"How do you mean?"

"Oh, my job and so on. It makes me a kind of professional corrupter of the young. Lee can tell you." The boy suggested that they drink to this profession, and the young instructor was pressed to go further.

"I teach them English is all," he continued, "and the pay-off they finally get to is a kind of corruption, because what they learn, when they've had the full treatment, is nothing about any particular book or any particular author or period so much as something fairly unnerving about life."

"Life," echoed Lee sonorously to a boy who had stopped near them for an instant before passing on.

"Whatever do you mean?" Elizabeth questioned Steitler with mock dismay.

"I mean that what they learn, if nothing worse, is that there's more to it all than this lovely, green place out here, than the society of their kind, these princelings and their young ladies. What they learn from me is that they're never going to have it so good again; that the great ones, the ones they read, saw it all as pretty black. I'm nothing, you see, if not trite, but what really gets me is the sense that I'm instructing a lot of beautiful, healthy children in the use of crutches, which at this point in their career is a morbid and rather pointless lesson. I can tell them seven times every time we meet that in a few years they're going to break their legs and need the crutches I'm offering now, but they don't believe it and, so help me, at moments like these, I really don't myself."

"And neither do I!" said Elizabeth. Lee laughed and turned to his friend.

Although slightly nearsighted, Elizabeth, so that noth‾ing might damage the charm of her dark brown eyes, tragic and wide apart under straight brows, wore no glasses but carried instead a miniature lorgnette, for which she now searched in her purse, unobtrusively and on her lap so that Steitler, who was speaking to her son, would not notice. She found them and peered through them at him, seeing him clearly for the first time—his face sharp as a razor with a large, straight nose and eyes, small and inquisitive. Medieval, she thought, without asking herself why, but remembering some fourteenth-century panel, from the Cloisters perhaps, that bore the likeness of such a face. Only his mouth, which was cunning to the corners, where it lost itself in a kind of humor, and his hair, dark and heavy, digressed from what she would have considered otherwise a chilling purpose. She was unable to tell, nor could she well remember now, his height, but she guessed him tall, as tall at least as her son, who, like his father before him, stood over six feet. She listened to him speak as he looked up at the bare ribs of the umbrella above them. His way of talking interested her: like a boy trying to talk like a teacher or, perhaps more justly, like a teacher trying to talk like a boy. It was his use of the highly colloquial or simply the ungrammatical expression that fascinated her in particular, for in neither case, clearly, did he speak in such a manner out of ignorance of the more elegant expression but, rather, by some design. This design, it struck her, was to seem altogether straightforward and natural, but its ultimate effect upon his listeners was quite the opposite, for his constant avoidance of anything approaching elegant or sophisticated language grew to appear a far greater elegance or sophistication itself. His was the role almost of the eighteenth-century courtier playing at being a shepherd, and there was in it much the same brittle, old-fashioned charm. And that was, perhaps, part of his design too. At any rate she decided him to be very clever, knew him to be very attractive. When he lowered his glance, she placed her lorgnette on the table behind her glass.

From the next table, which flaunted a red and purple umbrella, arose the shrill laugh of a girl and in a moment the girl herself. She put her tanned arms with their spirals of silver bracelets on the shoulders of a boy who sat with his back to them, and kissed him on the nape of his neck. He reached out to take hold of her, but she slipped away and caught sight of the three who watched her.

"Three cheers," she said, and laughed again. Leander was the first to turn away, and in a moment she reached their table and leaned upon it, brushing the hair from her eyes and looking slowly at each of them. When she reached Steitler, she stopped.

"Hi," he said.

"Hi . . ." The boy whom she had kissed called to her, but she did not hear him.

"What can we do you for?" Steitler looked at Elizabeth as he spoke.

"I don't know . . ." She rested there briefly, smelling sweetly of a perfume that was familiar to all of them and of the freshly ironed dress she wore. Elizabeth picked up her glass and sipped from it.

"Why don't each of you three little cheers give me your cherries?" asked the girl.

"Sure," Leander fished one out for her. Steitler did the same, and she took them both.

"How about you?"

Elizabeth replied by holding her glass forward. "I've already eaten mine, I'm afraid."

"Meany," said the girl, "but take this anyway." She offered a yellow rose that was fastened to her belt. "Here." Elizabeth took it and was about to thank her when the boy from the next table came over and, wrapping his arms about her waist, told her that everyone was crying for her.

"Oh, the poor babies," she said, almost as if she would weep, turning to look at her friend who stood just behind her. Then she turned from him and laughed. "I'm not tight."

"Of course not," said Steitler

"Don't you really think so?" she asked.

"Not on your life," answered Leander.

"Well you're a silly, a real silly then." She looked at Elizabeth. "I guess I have to go now." She reached out and shook hands as the boy started to draw her away. "So long!" she called over her shoulder as she left, "and thank you."

"Good-bye," said Elizabeth, "and thank *you.*" The girl's reply was obscured by the acclaim with which she was received once more beneath the red and purple umbrella.

"Well, you got the rose, Mrs. Poor," said Steitler.

"Isn't it lovely," Elizabeth held it out so that they all could see, concealing herself behind it. The sun was lower now, a corner of it only burning through the angle the tower made with the little hill.

"Tight," Leander took the rose and turned it about slowly. "She was plastered."

"Oh, well," said Steitler, "it's Saturday—the weekend."

"Good heavens, so it is. And George's lecture, I'd almost forgotten."

"We've lots of time before then, Mother."

Elizabeth was glad that there was lots of time. She breathed deeply and reached out for the rose. Steitler returned it to her, and, as if that were a signal, the chimes in the tower across the golf course started to ring.

"Oh Lord!" said Leander. Steitler laughed.

"Just like a music box."

"A Gothic music box," the young instructor answered her, "and such is college." They were silent while the chimes played a number of melodies including Brahms' *Lullaby* and *America the Beautiful*, and the waiter returned to replace their glasses.

CHAPTER

VI

IN THE city the light of late afternoon filled Emma Plaut's bedroom where she sat reading the paper. Bone had gone out after lunch and, though she had been momentarily annoyed at not learning his destination, her good humor was restored when he told her that, since he would not return for dinner, she might have the rest of the day to herself. She had decided to spend this time in the comfort of her room, reading. She was a little woman much given to facial expressions of worried doubt, but when her eyes rested upon the complexities of German print it was as though someone had placed a kind hand on each of her shoulders, and her face would assume a serenity intense enough to encourage the advances of the most timid of the pigeons that she fed when she walked in the park. It was a curiously unwrinkled face, though she was deeper in middle age than her employer, and only one line between her eyes could be easily noticed. This seemed more of a crease than a line, as if at night she removed her countenance and folded it away in her bureau drawer among sweet-smelling handkerchiefs.

Rocking lightly in her chair, enjoying the late sun, warm as a scarf, on the back of her neck, she read her paper as carefully as always, omitting no article however obscure, when suddenly she stopped rocking, and the crease between her eyes deepened. Something fearful on the third page had caught her attention: a small paragraph hidden beneath an advertisement for foot liniment. It appeared that there was a statue of Goethe in the park. Familiar only with the section near Bone's apartment, she had not known this, nor did she know any more of Goethe than his name and the fact that he was a poet, a poet "long beloved of the German people" as the article announced, but what she read of him, or of his statue, angered her so greatly that she discovered a greater love for him than she had previously suspected. The statue had fallen victim in a recent and trifling anti-German demonstration led by some college students and was presently "outrageously defaced with paint."

In no time at all she knew what she must do. Taking off her apron, she hung it on a peg behind the door, and from a curtained closet drew the dress she wore on her days off— a navy-blue one with pearl buttons running all the way down the front. With small, angry movements and some indecipherable muttering, she put it on, changed into her narrow street shoes with buckles, and clapped on her straw hat that bore a red cloth rose fastened to its band. Then out into the kitchen where she found some lye soap and a scrub brush. These she placed in a metal pail that she slipped over her arm like a sunbonnet. She was about to leave by the back door when she remembered a towel, found it, said something inappropriate to Simon, who had heard the noise and came out to watch, and then left, slamming the door.

"Well, Emma," said the back elevator man as they rode down to the street, "out for a spree? Du bist outgeganging, hey?"

"Oh, spree you, fresh!" she muttered. "What a business!" and in a few minutes she was out on the street corner waiting for a bus.

The newspaper had given only the approximate location of her statue, and when she reached the lower part of the park she realized that she had no clear idea as to exactly where to go. It was a lovely day, however, and she found an empty bench and sat down upon it to consider her problem and rest, placing the pail on the ground between her feet. With her eyes she avoided the pigeons for whom she had brought no crumbs this time. She was overheated from her activity, already the pail had grown heavy and the insides of her fingers red from its handle, she had lost something of her original determination, and for an unspeakable moment she was afraid that she might burst into tears. But there were the curious glances of the passers-by, and there were the pigeons. She straightened her back and then her hat, fluffed out the stitched petals of the rose and dried away what had been the beginnings of a tear. A light wind blew and cooled her. She felt better. The crisis was passed, and she had enjoyed it fiercely. There was nothing now to do but find the statue and remove from it the paint.

But where to go? She wondered about this as best she could, her thought obstructed by visions of what the statue of the poet must look like, until she caught sight of a green-clad park attendant. Picking up her pail, she walked across a little bridge and asked cautiously, naming no names, if he knew the whereabouts of any statue nearby. If he guessed her motives, he gave no evidence of it, but only pointed to the tunnel under a green bank and told her that if she followed that path for a little way she would come at last to a kind of open square where there were, he believed, some such things. She thanked him in her best English.

There were children in the tunnel.

"Hullo!" they shouted. The curved stone wall returned their greeting.

"Who's afraid!" yelled a little blonde girl, and the end of her question bounced back at her. The others fell in love with this and kept shouting it. It was dark in there, some rainwater still lay in a shallow pool, and Emma was glad to come out into the sudden greenness on the other side. The path branched off in two directions, which confused her, but one of them was smaller and prettier than the other, and she decided that that one would be right.

It led down past a weathered green rotunda whose sheltered exterior would protect until later in the spring the deserted carousel within and echoed now indistinctly the patter of Emma's shoes on the uneven pavement as she proceeded up an even narrower lane bordered with forsythia not yet deceived into bloom. Finding herself at the approach of sunset with no other living figure in sight except an occasional squirrel or bird, she gave a little exclamation of incredulity at coming suddenly upon the square she had been promised. Surrounding her in sculptured detachment stood the disembodied heads and shoulders of a minor senate of the great. In their center, larger than life-size, a stone warrior sat astride his imperious charger. To each in turn she went, the pail hanging nearly forgotten in her hand. Into the composure of each stone face she peered for traces of the abomination she had come to remove, but in none could she find any. To the inscription on each pedestal she also turned, but there was no familiar name among them.

Almost it did not matter. Emma wondered if perhaps she were not dreaming. The section of the park into which her search had led her was rich in obscurity. Its only entrance was the path by which she had come, and trees and bushes sheltered it on every side. The late sun sifted in long bands through the complicity of spring leaves and fell like honey upon the new grass and the gray stone. Emma took the towel out of her pail, spread it out on the warrior's pedestal, and sat down upon it. Then she removed her hat and, placing it beside her, leaned her head against the supple flank of the stone charger and fell asleep. The only sound was the sound of the unhurried wind.

Slipping almost imperceptibly at first from the part of the statue against which she leaned, she listed farther and farther to the side until her navy-blue dress was pulled all crooked, and the row of pearl buttons ran diagonally from her shoulder to the hem of her skirt which was itself twisted up to her knee. She balanced perilously there for a few more minutes, then lurched and fell back to awake with a start and grab up at the horse, catching hold of his genitals that hung like ripe stone apples above her. She righted herself. How long has it been, she wondered.

It could not have been long, for the sun had not yet disappeared. She noticed, however, that there were pigeons now, stalking, with little electric movements of the head and neck, upon the grass. *Ach*, she thought, *der Goethe*. Replacing the towel in the pail and picking up her hat which had fallen with its rose to the ground, she stood up and resumed her search. *Ach*, she thought. It was late. The path led her through the trees and out of the square, and she continued walking until she found herself among people once more. Spying out another park attendant, she asked her veiled questions once again and was directed back to the place whence she had just come. She thanked him politely and made the gesture of following his advice but, as soon as he seemed not to be watching any longer, started up a rather steep incline in yet another direction.

"Well, well, well," said a voice, "and here we are."

Emma looked up with such speed that she had to catch hold of the hand-rail to prevent herself from falling. Over the crest of the hill that she climbed, there arose, immense and dark like a great wave about to curl over and crash down upon her, the solitary figure of Tristram Bone. The saffron sky, feathered with frayed red clouds and uncanny strips of pale green, flamed up like the end of the world behind him.

"Mr. Bone," she cried out in confusion and then, regaining her composure, ascended towards him.

CHAPTER

VII

BEHIND the inn what little light there was left seemed to devour everything except the bright dresses of the girls and the voices. Elizabeth, with the two young men on either side of her, leaned far back in her chair as she spoke through the dusk.

"It's a lovely place," she said to them, "and it's been years for me, you know."

"Has it changed a great deal?" Lee echoed the young instructor's question to his mother who appeared not to have heard.

"Well, I can't remember really," she answered, "because that was a hundred years ago. I guess it has." The liquor was not without its effect on her. "But the people haven't. I would have known that girl, the one with the rose, anywhere for instance, and even you," she paused, "Paul— I don't think I knew any of the teachers then, but I imagine they were all very much like you, only older in their way. There weren't any chimes here then, but we

72

used to bring phonographs out on the lawn, I think it was
here, and dance to them. The roaring twenties, you know.
Flappers and flivvers and flaming youth. Neither of you
would remember it."

"Well, that's charming of you to say," answered Steitler,
"but I certainly do—not from here, but the disease
spread."

"Disease?"

"The lovely, giddy, green disease of this place, this sweet
and dangerous hospital that nobody wants to leave—ever."

"Not *dangerous*," she replied to him, "but *safe*, safe as a
house."

"Ah, ha, there you are!"

"Pooh, pooh, pooh," she finished, smiling. "What is
your home?" she then asked, irrelevantly, but as though
the question had been long in her mind, and he came very
close to telling her—of course the facts, the state, the
town, its geographic relation to other towns she knew
nearby, but almost more than that: such as how the twenties roared under Spanish moss in a small Florida town
that had somehow missed the land boom there, and how
youth had flamed among the Baptists. By means of the
yellow umbrella that sheltered them where they sat from
nothing now but the greater part of a spring moon, he
indicated to them why children, why he as a child, were
happy as it is said, and, by requesting that they lean back
far enough so as to observe the sky above them, demon-
strated the depth or height of whatever it is that takes the

place of such a happiness. From time to time he would pause that they might not by any single voice be drawn away to overlook the common music, not so much Mendelssohn now, he suggested, as Sousa perhaps, and wondered, as he paused, whether it were not indeed more difficult to be articulate than to be—in the sky that cried down for a great bird—a great fish or a yellow rose so splendid as to put the moon to fright.

A cigarette. At last Elizabeth asked for one, was given it, forgot who lit it for her, and decided to herself that if one were to take all the clothes off Paul Steitler it would be noticeable to no one farther away from him than Leander, so deep had the twilight become.

"Oh my," she said, "will you look what time it is!"

"You look, will you, Lee?" said Steitler. "I'm embarrassed." It was late, too late to have supper before Motley's lecture, they agreed, too late in fact for anything but to finish what was left in their three glasses and then to proceed across the campus to the building where Elizabeth's friend was to speak.

"You know," she said, "I can hardly wait. I've no idea how he'll be with such a large audience. He always does wonderfully at Tristram's, Tristram Bone's, you know, Lee, but of course there are never half so many there."

"What sort of a person is he, Mrs. Poor," asked Steitler, "as a friend, I mean?"

Elizabeth burst into laughter. "I don't know why that's so amusing," she said, laughing with equal delight again, "but it is." She grew serious once more. "He's very nice, an awfully pleasant person really, but very little and sandy, and there's something so innocent about him. You know I can think of one very unattractive phrase that I once heard him use himself about someone else that would pretty much sum up all his bad points—not because he used it, if you see what I mean, but because it applies to him too. But no; it's too horrid." She was urged to have no such scruples.

"Well then," she continued, "he's the kind of a person who looks in his handkerchief after he has blown his nose." Leander gave a look of exaggerated horror and Steitler laughed. "Well, I warned you," she said, "and that will give you entirely the wrong idea about him and I'm sorry I said it because he's charming and kind and generous. But anyway, you'll both see him soon because we're to meet him right after the lecture."

"I wonder how many of these people will be there," said Steitler, looking around the terrace, which was considerably emptier than when they had arrived. "It should be quite an audience with any luck at all."

"Well, he's used to that," answered Elizabeth. "And it must make it easier anyway, like talking to children."

As they got up to leave, Steitler bumped his head against the umbrella causing the wooden pole that held it to collapse in the middle where it was hinged. The ribbed canvas top fell with a clatter to the table, missing Elizabeth and Leander who had already risen, but sweeping everything to the ground. Most startling was the sudden wealth of sky that it revealed, like coming out of a tunnel, but almost equally so the noise of it, which acted as a signal for one last symphonic crescendo from those still left sitting there in the darkness. The terrace resounded with laughter, hoots, and loud words eager to be heard above the general din, and the white coat of a waiter flickered its way from the bar to where they stood. Elizabeth walked away to the door of the inn, where she awaited the two men. In a moment they joined her. Steitler apologized, Elizabeth laughed forgiveness, and Leander opened the door for them. They paused in the dimly lit lobby where Steitler, with more apologies, returned to Elizabeth her lorgnette, one of whose lenses was badly cracked and the other missing altogether, and she protested its unimportance, swore there was nothing more worth seeing anyway and, to put an end to his penitence, declared that she was rather cool and asked Lee if he would mind running up to her room and bringing down her coat. He appeared not to mind at all and before long she was helped into a light spring one of the palest pink and ready to start with them on their way.

"Oh, by the way," said Lee, "here's your rose. It escaped somehow or other."

"Oh dear," she said, "I won't be able to smell it without my glasses."

"Ah, but we will," said Steitler, and as they left she fastened it to her collar.

It was unfortunate to begin with that the professor chosen to introduce Motley was the possessor of a full beard, and a muffled hiss of "Beaver" from the rear of the capacious lecture hall occasioned some wild and somewhat less muffled laughter among those undergraduates and their young ladies not early enough to have obtained a closer view of this scholar, who appeared to be something of a favorite among them. Knowing themselves unable to suppress for long the bulk of their mirth, they strained to catch the glimmer, however faint, of whatever humor there might be in his introduction so that their laughter might not appear altogether unseemly, and it was not long before their patience was rewarded. He spoke of the distinguished Mr. Motley from whom one had been fortunate, during the last decade, in hearing frequently, of one's consequent indebtedness to him and also of his indebtedness to the literary tradition that had itself drawn often from the ranks of the university which was honored with his presence this evening as it had not, unfortunately, been similarly honored during Mr. Motley's undergraduate days. The bearded professor with painful cunning then consented to clap the dénouement on what even the dullest of his listeners recognized as preliminary to a vast and panoramic jest by declaiming with studied gravity the name of George Motley's alma mater, in short, the rival university. He was answered with uproarious laughter from the rear of the hall, a few boos at the name of the hated institution, and scattered applause throughout. After a brief period of some triumph he pronounced the celebrated visitor's name for the last time, smiled hairily, and bowed Motley to his position of prominence before the audience.

"I thank you," he said. "Members of the faculty, ladies and gentlemen." To those few who knew him it became immediately apparent that he was at his best, and to those who did not, merely his appearance, as contrasted with that of the gentleman who had introduced him, was a pleasure, for at approximately the same point in space where the bottom-most hair of the professor's beard had hung gleamed now the balding, freckled scalp of the novelist; and there were few who watched him who did not recollect, articulately or otherwise, that, as when one visits the zoo, it is often most rewarding to save the smaller, more complicated animals until last.

"I have come here to talk to you this evening about a matter that has always occupied a great deal of my time, but before I begin I would like to tell you a little story that may serve both to illustrate my point and also," he turned to the professor, "to help you forget the more unfortunate circumstances of my earlier years" (moderate laughter) "which, you must believe me, were more or less out of my control." (More of the same.) "Now it seems there was a rabble-rouser once, an anarchist if you will, who was in the habit of taking his tea in one of those parks where anarchy and the like are the subjects of much extemporaneous oratory. Well, one day as he sat there, on his favorite red bench, a heretofore inoffensive bird sprang up nearby

and, as it flew above the anarchist, released a soupçon or
two of dropping on his head and then flew off again. Our
friend examined the damage to his ensemble, shook a
heavy, guttural fist at the retreating bird, and snarled
angrily: 'For the rich you sing!' " The story was highly successful, and undergraduate approval was conveniently
summarized by a youth sitting in front of Steitler who
wrote in his notebook, "Motley is a good egg." Motley was
also a good speaker, and instead of allowing the laughter to
die he caught up his discourse while it was still almost impossible to be heard.

"Now that story," he continued, "the way I have told
it to you, is a matter of politics more or less, but like all
stories it is what I am going to call an open symbol—by
which I mean that the same story can be applied to most
any other field. Clearly enough, the three main symbols
here, the man and the bird of whose talents singing is
one, are not inherently political. The entire fabric can be
changed if we simply do not call the man an anarchist,
who would of course by nature curse the rich, but call him
instead someone else who would be more interested in
cursing some other group. Let us, for instance, call him an
unsuccessful writer, or at least a young and struggling
one, and let us say that what he curses are the successful
writers whom he considers inferior. Perhaps now we will
better understand each other and I am nearer than ever
to my subject.

"What is this young man saying when he curses the bird

for not singing? He is saying that the cards are against him, that, given the proper opportunities, the song of the bird in this case, he could make something of it. And what can we tell him right away? Why we can tell him that he can make something out of what the bird did give him, I mean that from the bird, the symbol of his personal experience, he can—with the help of imagination—distill as much as others can from what is perhaps a richer experience."

"This is really fantastic," whispered Steitler to Lee, who sat next to him. "Can he know what he's saying?" Leander shrugged without taking his eyes from the platform. Motley continued.

"I would like the young writers in the audience this evening to consider my story in that light—to put themselves in the place of the young man sitting on the park bench waiting, as we all must wait, for whatever happens to fall our way. I would like them to understand that from this story, as a story and not a parable, it is possible to fashion anything from a Divine Comedy to a short story in any one of the *hausfrau* magazines."

Elizabeth found it nearly impossible to keep her mind fixed on the words of her friend, and heard what she heard only dimly through a mist of recollection and anticipation that prevented, at this moment, her more detailed attention. It was not until the novelist had started to tell another story that she was enabled by her curiosity to wrest herself from cluttered observations of the multitude of young faces about her. He was telling, she realized slowly, a tale that she had heard before and recently, a myth he called it, about a king and two sisters.

"But a myth," he continued, "whether it's the last echo of an old reality or just the current translation of something that never happened at all, is nevertheless composed, like everything else, of facts, edible, nourishing facts that can be put to almost any use you choose. Here for instance, as I have said, we have a king named Tireus, who married a princess named Procne. And there is our beginning. Many of you will know the tale already, but I propose to tell it once more for purposes that I hope may become clear as I go along. They lived together, you see," he proceeded, as though the utterance caused him a kind of pain, "happily and at peace, this royal pair, and if there was no flaming love between them, there was at least a pleasant and mutual dependence, pleasant and mutual enough, that is, to result, after a little, in the birth of a son whom they called Itys." The little novelist wiped his forehead and replaced the handkerchief in his breast pocket, whence it protruded in starched petals like a rare flower. "And all went well until Procne, lonely and perhaps a trifle bored with the life of a queen, asked if her sister, Philomela, might be brought to her from the land where they had lived together as girls. Stop here a minute and consider the beauty of recognizing as current the last brittle vibrations of an ancient situation set spinning, like a coin, ages ago!" His eyes were wide, and he extended his hands far out to either side as though proffering on a broad salver for all to see the peculiar significance of what he was saying. "From her loneliness and tedium she fashioned this request, and her husband, Tireus himself, set sail to do her bidding.

"It was on the voyage home that he fell in love with the beautiful Philomela—somewhat younger and more beautiful, we suspect, than her sister, Procne—and, because she would not willingly return his love, he ravished her one night aboard the darkened ship. And then, that she might never betray his guilt, he had her tongue cut out. Upon reaching his own country again, he sent the unhappy Philomela to live with an obscure and understanding old woman, and told his wife that her sister had fallen ill and died on the return voyage. Philomela, however, though she could not speak, wove the tale of her sorrow into a tapestry which she was able by stealth to have taken to Procne. Procne understood instantly all that had happened, stole her sister secretly into the palace, and together they plotted how they might best revenge themselves upon the heartless king. Imagine this scene."

Motley paused here to sip from the glass of water provided him, and to gauge, if he could, the attention of his audience. Steitler glanced over at Elizabeth, who gazed straight before her with unseeing curiosity.

"Even as the sisters were occupied with these plans of theirs—sitting fearfully in some sunless place—who should enter before them but Itys, the little son of Tireus and

Procne. It became clear at that very instant that the most perfect revenge would be to kill the boy and, as was the custom then, to serve him up for his father's dinner. And so they did. When Tireus had eaten of the unholy dish, the sisters named its contents to him, and his grief and anger were so great, their revenge so complete, that he tore down from the wall a mighty sword and pursued them across the barren plains of his windy land. When they feared they could flee no farther and were certain of capture and death by the sword they saw flashing behind them, they fell to their knees and prayed to the gods to deliver them somehow from the dangers and sorrow of a life they could no longer face. Their prayers were heard, and, before the maddened king had quite reached them, all three were transformed into birds, a nightingale, a sparrow, and a hawk, to fly screaming into the blue sky.

"Now for the facts of the marriage between Procne and Tireus, the cutting out of Philomela's tongue, the killing of Itys and the eating of him by his own father, and the final metamorphosis into birds—for these facts, for these open symbols if you prefer, substitute what more currently plausible equivalents you will. And at the same time, if you will indulge me for only a few more minutes (I'm not so old as to be unaware of the other lures awaiting you this evening) I will suggest several possibilities that have, in this direction, occurred to . . ."

The story itself did not particularly interest Elizabeth, but she was curious still as to when and from whom she

had heard it before. Not until a few minutes more had
passed, and Motley's voice was again no more than a
wordless humming in her ears, did she remember that it
was Tristram's tale, the one he had told her in a somewhat
broken and distorted form the previous evening. For a
little time she marveled at this, and soon then she forgot it.

Whatever had been conceived during the afternoon on
the lawn behind the inn, on other smaller lawns elsewhere
in the town, and in countless undergraduate rooms where
by the clever light admitted through the mullioned case-
ment windows even larger quantities of liquor were con-
sumed by the students and their young ladies—whatever
was conceived then and in those places was, at the conclusion of Motley's lecture, nearer birth than ever. They had
gone to hear him even in the midst of their revelry not
only because he was famous among them and represented a
level of success for which each felt himself or herself still a
candidate, but because one of the principal rules in the
great and friendly game of a college weekend was: to keep
moving. Both sexes fought on the same side towards the
same end, which was male victory or female capitulation
depending upon which named it, and the common enemy
was recognized by both as boredom or, in less tragic terms,
as merely the state of having nothing in particular to do
next. The rule was consequently to continue proceeding
from one externally organized situation to another until
finally one might be reached that fitted exactly and pre-

cluded defeat. This could scarcely be expected to come about until late, and Motley's lecture was therefore not an interruption so much as a necessary interlude in the play. When he brought it to a lively close, the audience prepared to depart as enthusiastically as it had arrived something less than an hour earlier. Throats were dry, lungs thirsted for cigarette smoke, and Motley, by finishing, became for them the small boy running onto the field with the bucket, the damp towel, and shrill encouragement, and the applause he received was great.

Once outside he easily found Elizabeth and her two young men, who stood just off the path that ran past the lecture hall and rang now with the footfalls, shuffling laughter, and talk of those who had lately been his audience.

"And you came!" he exclaimed, rushing up to her and clasping her hand. "Bless you, bless you, bless you! And this—don't tell me—is Lee!" he continued, placing his short arm around Steitler's shoulders. "And this—?" He looked with mock helplessness at Lee.

"Is the real Lee?" offered Elizabeth.

"You lie, you lie!" he said high above their laughter, "I know it, but I love it. So be it, this then is Lee."

Elizabeth introduced him to them both and congratulations were exchanged—for George on his lecture, Elizabeth on her rose and keen perception, Lee and Steitler on simply being who they were. Another group of about six couples came up and was presented to the novelist. The boys were classmates of Lee's for the most part, and the girls, belonging one to each, stood in pretty and vocal admiration of the novelist, who shook their hands with smiles and quick nods of his head. Steitler recognized one of them as the girl they had encountered earlier at the inn, and whispered his discovery to Elizabeth as Motley entertained the others. She received the information silently and, without turning to her informant, smiled recognition. In a moment the girl observed them and came over.

"Hi again." She laughed. "Isn't this lovely. My name's Hope." They talked. Lee approached and was taken up into their conversation. Motley continued to dominate the larger group and little by little the passing crowd disappeared down the path leaving them all alone there by the empty lecture hall.

The night was warm and clear as dark water. Steitler looked up at it, shut his eyes to the stars for a moment, and realized that he still felt the effect of his cocktails. He wished for another and with a curious pang of excitement guessed that so, probably, did the others. The others. They were young, and they were mostly beautiful, and this was part of his excitement. Elizabeth, who stood nearest him, was not any the less so.

This was an interim, a little stopping between lengths of going on, and he savored it by watching her beside him there as she talked generally, vaguely, to those whose youth seemed with her more of a lovely disadvantage than otherwise. Among them was the girl who had come to them that afternoon for cherries, the girl named Hope. Only Elizabeth had been unable to give her one, had had no cherry then to offer Hope before her now, as earlier, in fresh lemon-colored cotton and ballet slippers, questioning, receiving whatever there might be to receive. There was a good deal, from Elizabeth at first, about how the night was too warm for pink coats even, pink coats too pink for yellow roses, and then more from Lee. When he had started to speak, she turned and caught Steitler's glance. The excitement grew in him.

"There will be years and years and years," Steitler said, "and then a moment. And then years and years and years again."

"What kind of a moment?"

"I don't know." He was sincere. "Only a moment. There was one just now."

"Oh," she said. "Seriously?"

"Sure."

She looked at him carefully as though through her little lorgnette that he had broken. There seemed to her too much face to take in even at several more casual glances . . . at least she had failed to. It looked lean and complicated like an insect's but, after all, a dark and splendid insect's. She remembered to smile. It was early for comparisons, but she felt herself on the point of making them.

"In another moment," she said, raising her eyebrows, "I'll go."

"Whatever for?"

"For I'm sick of standing here."

He made a move forward as though to start them all on their way somewhere or anywhere when Motley and a short girl with hair redder than his turned to them and announced that it was decided. They would go down to the lake. Elizabeth took Steitler's arm.

CHAPTER

VIII

"I AM WRITING this on the terrace where the sun is making a burning-glass of my spectacles so no more at present although I have much more I could say." Maroo looked up as though to verify this, then signed the letter to her grandson, Leander Poor, and slipped it under her knitting bag away from the light wind. Much more indeed.

The low, shingled house lay in a small valley defined by a ridge of pines and a long hill, which together drew all of a rough circle about it except for one absent arc and the view it gave of the Blue Ridge mountains, Whiteoak, Skyuga, Hogback, which the terrace faced. The old lady sat there alone, no other house nor any other person in sight, and looked out over the short lawn where a tulip tree beckoned at her. Above, the round sky was blue as a toy and the afternoon sun bright on the red clay of the driveway. She removed her spectacles and leaned her head back so that only the sky was visible.

The chair she sat in was of wicker with an enormous

fan-shaped wicker back and a stiff wicker skirt to hide its
legs. Next to it, on a low round table, lay a small silver
coffer, and from it and from her white linen dress the light
reflected brilliantly, giving her bright prominence against
the gray front of the house, the terrace's dull red brick,
and the dark green of the boxwood that bordered it on two
sides. It was as if she had sat against the great unfurled
back of her chair giddily at first on what was for a time a
mountain, and that the mountain then, encouraged by
the placid brightness of the linen, silver, wicker of the ancient figure, had sunk slowly down to become a valley
for her stronghold. And it was as if she had not noticed
this, or had pretended not to, but passed the descent by
writing letters and observing the world about her not in
terms alone of the danger of mountains and the strength
of valleys but as a whole diverse and ordered geography.

She put her spectacles back on and reread the letter to
her grandson. Though his letters to her were very scarce,
never more than one every two months or so, and short
then, no real answer to hers, she wrote to him more frequently than to anyone else. She wrote him—the letter she
reread now was a good example—charmingly and at
length about this small North Carolina town and the people it had attracted from the most implausible localities
the world over, and about herself in relation to them. Her
way with him was always to write with a full knowledge
of the figure she cut among them, of herself as but another
person from another implausible locality with a great

age to distinguish her where others had, no less pictur-
esquely, some other gentle lunacy like drink, or hurt and
petulant ambition, a love of the hunt that flourished there,
or merely an inertia making departure from those pretty
mountains nigh unthinkable. Each made impositions and
was imposed upon to the extent permitted by the nature
and width of the almost inevitable crack wigwagging to
all intents visibly through him, and for her, with a crack
of age running around rather than through, impositions
were endless both ways, received and imparted. "They talk
to me," she had written, "as they would to a drunk or a
child, thinking, I daresay, that the old citizen isn't what
she once was and that they had therefore best jolly her
along. My reward, of course, is that I can then talk to them
as though I *were* a drunk or a child and that keeps me
busy. They eat it up." She went on then to write of what
concerned her now, the imminent arrival of Miss Mary
Curtis, a near contemporary, as near as one comes this side
of the grave she suggested, on foot up the twisted red clay
drive, to read French with her for an hour or two. The
consensus was, she proceeded, that Mary, who had seen
better days than most, was not "all there," but if this were
true it only served to accentuate the splendor of the relic.
Nor had a certain lack of speculation in her pale old eye
anything to do with the way she could read the French
plays they enjoyed together of an afternoon. "Tristram,"
she had written, "who knows a good thing when he sees it,
was charmed by her while he was here. He, by the way,

is a good lad and I am fond of him." She released these thoughts freely but never forgetting to whom it was they were directed.

No fissure scarred or weakened Leander Poor, she knew, for he was in his youth as invulnerable quite as she, with the difference only that his was of an untutored sort to be tested weekly with her letters, confronted with her carefully selected thoughts and tales of people and ways which might mark him as theirs and chip in him a treacherous understanding as soon as he should show interest in them as heretofore he had not. If it were possible to imagine fear as ever being her motive, then it could be that she was afraid for the boy as of or for nothing else. It could be then that she wrote, wrote him letters never to be answered even to himself, somehow to guard him from just such a sorcery as hers—hers by default of age, harmless now to her with an old heart pumping, pumping blood through an old mind.

Could he only become accustomed to danger, to the sense that to be alive was perilous, as the quaint fiction of an old lady, might he then not come to see the acts of fear or their possibility as a fiction too; yet all this must be done humorously, quaintly, in just the ways least likely to reach him, for otherwise he might pay too much heed and think of the old citizen as the rat about to leave the sinking ship, to sink gratefully through that last rat-hole. Oh what a delicate game the old rat could be imagined to be playing, scuttling along through wreckage and broken things, trying to make no noise, to reach a goal not to be reached too quickly or decisively but with subterfuge and stealth, to point out the trap yet pretend not to notice it. Yet at the same time, this might not be the game at all.

One felt she did not need a motive but could act as directly and deftly as she reached for a cigarette from the silver box at her side; could write him, perhaps, not for her pleasure, her need or concern, but because there were letters to write as there were cigarettes to be smoked, and because this was a part of what was left her. The only certainty was that she did not need as did Tristram Bone, as did Emma Plaut, to register herself somewhere with someone; did not need a reliable witness, impartial as a mirror but able to retain what it reflected, and, by seeing everything, somehow to justify everything, absolve her from whatever guilt, qualify her for whatever prize.

She read on to the conclusion of her letter and was brought up short by her words about the sun making a burning-glass of her spectacles. It had been just so, and was still. She had much more she could say. Not at present . . .

At her side now there stood the colored man whom she employed to do odd jobs about the house. She had not noticed his approach and gave a little exclamation to discover him so close. He thrust out a tubular pink tongue and laughed hoarsely.

"It's them birds," he said. "Want 'em let out again to-night, Mis' Caven?"

They were white pigeons bought by Lee when he had been down several summers before with his mother, and Maroo had kept them on in what used to have been a chicken coop behind the house. For fear that hawks might get them they were released only once every day or so to fly themselves into a kind of murmuring fatigue and then be readmitted into their cage. The colored man, however, was not eager that they be so exercised every day because occasionally they stayed out rather longer than usual, until close to sundown perhaps, and he was obliged to await their return before going home himself. Maroo was aware of this, but her afternoon on the terrace had set her to thinking in terms of a high and cloudless sky and she therefore insisted, suggesting that tomorrow it might be well to keep them in. He assented with a great show of amused unconcern and had started to go when he remembered something and turned around.

"I saw lil Mis' Curtis on her way up the road. I 'spect she'll be here in a jiffy—huffin' and puffin' . . ." He disappeared around the boxwoods adding in an undertone, "She'll blow your house *down*."

Her way was slower than he had guessed, and Maroo had time to reenter the house, shuffle the dogwood that arose in a horizontal spray from a Chinese bowl, and smoke a cigarette from one of her white paper holders. The blue screen of smoke trembled in the still air of the living-room, catching the sun as it listed through the broad picture window giving out upon the terrace, the tulip tree, and the mountains beyond. By and by Miss Curtis arrived in much the condition that had been anticipated. She was one of the very few who called Maroo by her true name, Juliette—the other having been invented by her grandchildren in their inarticulate infancy and reserved now only for them—and she greeted her by it now. Maroo, who used first names with her contemporaries as rarely as she heard her own, responded with a gracious "Mary."

Miss Curtis looked imperfectly preserved from another age. Her eyes were wide and pale, and she had the earnest, bulging forehead associated with dwarfs, the little figures in the foreground of Velásquez court scenes not tall enough to conceal a Hapsburg or the painter himself broodingly reflected somewhere behind them in a mirror, nor was she tall enough to obscure the top of Skyuga behind her. Her hair had long ago been red, one guessed from the hectic remnants that strayed beneath the dull green felt hat that matched her clay-stained walking shoes. Although it was her turn to reply, she stood silently for quite a few minutes against the window, looking at Maroo with a kind of complicity in her stance as though expecting from some recess about her person to hear a tiny alarm go off and give them both the proper signal. It sounded.

"And how nice to see you, my dear. *La porte est double ouverte*." Her accent was impeccable. "Oh . . . I have your mail here somewhere," she continued, rummaging in the pockets of her jacket. "Here. One, two, three. No, just one—these are mine." She retrieved the last two a little defensively from Maroo, who had taken them into her hand.

"Let's not read them now," suggested Maroo. She had glanced at hers and found it to be from Leander's college, but in a writing completely unfamiliar to her. That meant a more attentive reading than she was willing to give it with Mary Curtis there waiting.

"Oh good," she answered, "let's not indeed." Her breath came more evenly now, and she gave a smile so wide and open, her great eyes taking in the entire room and a part of the mountains towards which she had half turned, that it was as though she were seeing the world for the first time and might clap her hands to see it dance about her.

"Let's not read them now," she continued, "with all this . . ." She made a gesture so sweeping that she had to pivot her body like a discus-thrower to include in it both the living-room and the window. "Let's put them off . . ." She sat down as she spoke, resting her freckled hands on the chair arms and stretching out her green shod feet, as if she had concluded the subject, but only then to add warmly and intimately, "until some other time."

"A good idea," said Maroo, who scarcely felt any longer that it had been hers. "Did you remember to bring your Molière?"

"Yes," she replied. "Oh, and I saw the birds coming up." She said this gravely and yet casually as though perhaps she had not been intended to see them.

"The pigeons?"

"Yes, do they always fly like that, spinning around the valley in circles, one after the other, like a twirling rope?"

"They always do, around in circles, until they're tired, of course, and then they go sit in the trees."

"*So* beautiful," said Miss Curtis. "Might we take another look before starting?"

And so they went out, before starting, and stood on the lawn in front of the terrace to watch the white birds wing circles above them. Around and around they flew, not effortlessly, but speeding so fast that one imagined them chased by something, like lovers in a myth. But the pursuers were only each other, for they went, the six of them, in single file, not varying the distance between them and shining white in a sky so blue that it seemed almost miraculously not to dye them. The noise of their quick wings was like the tearing of paper, and somewhere there was danger in the spectacle.

Even as she stood there next to her friend, Maroo went beyond the experience and looked as though back upon it as something to be written of to Leander; an experience involving his pigeons and also Miss Curtis who assumed more than a mere spectator's role. She might well, herself, have been twirling the high cowboy rope to which the whizzing birds were sewn. Around and around they flew. She wondered about the letter awaiting her from someone she didn't know. The letter, the pigeons, Miss Mary Curtis, and, somewhere, beyond them, Leander, swung about the old lady but slower, and more slowly, as she gave them her thought, not to meet. The letter flew out at an angle to be picked up later and dealt with then, Miss Curtis and the birds settled down in different trees to woo one another from a distance, and only Leander remained, but swinging alone in a more distant circle, more remote than the mountains.

Once they were reestablished in the living-room and before they had an opportunity to begin their play, Miss Curtis had inquired about Mr. Bone, who had happened by during one of their readings several weeks before. Maroo replied that she had heard indirectly through her daughter, Elizabeth, that he had returned safely and was well.

"Such a very pleasant young man," Miss Curtis said dreamily.

"He was quite taken with you, you know."

"Yes," she replied, "I could tell. One *can* tell about such matters. But you see we had a good deal in common, your Mr. Bone and myself. Walking for one thing, a love of the promenade. He came up here on foot just as I did, though not in my company of course—he arriving later—and each very much in the face of certain disadvantages."

"I daresay that walking *is* no easy matter for him," conjectured Maroo. He had come dressed, like herself at this moment, in white, his large, closed face damp with the effort, but smiling, so that parts of heaviness had to shift position all about his mouth and eyes.

"No. He's so fat and I'm so old!" she laughed like a girl.

"And your road is *so* considerable. But the reward is always more than ample, my dear Juliette. Just those lovely birds! It must make a difference to be so big." She stretched her fingers out as far as they would reach along the arms of her chair as if to show the farthest extent of possible bigness for her.

"As far as walking is concerned, I'm sure. But you're altogether correct, and I have overheard him say that he is extremely fond of it."

"Yes, and as far as a great many things are concerned. Thinking, for instance. Oh just think about thinking through all that!"

Maroo laughed. "Everybody is always thinking something somewhere, through something."

"Oh you're right to be sure," came the answer. Then, more slowly, "Oh how very right you are," and little Miss Curtis twisted her amber beads carefully as though to turn off a kind of current as she gazed out of the window. Not so much the current of her thought as of a sudden feeling, perhaps, that there across the room was someone older by a little even than she. Older by a good deal if looks were any gauge. That ancient brown face, Mary Curtis seemed to say to herself, those ancient eyes heavy with age as though with sleep, but also as though irrecoverably awake to everything everybody was always thinking somewhere, through something. And there they probably were, were indeed had she turned to make certain, looking out at her only a little less ancient and difficult face, the amber eyes, the hectic hair, timorously burning in the late sun. It was as if Mary Curtis turned off the current of such feelings rather than of her thought as she twisted her beads, and turned it off only because it was too placid and bright to bear.

Soon after this they started to read their play, with Maroo, at Miss Curtis's suggestion, taking the male parts with her deep voice, and Miss Curtis those of the ladies. A good number of her better days having been spent in France, Miss Curtis spoke her lines with considerable authentic beauty, and Maroo matched her in ease and enthusiasm. They read *L'Avare*, acted it out, though sitting, with a kind of brittle fervor, so that the long room, littered here and there with sunlight on bright things, silver, porcelain, deft old eyes, knitting needles, seemed, in truth, peopled rather with seventeenth-century lovers and the miser they gulled, than with the old ladies sheltered there from the late afternoon sky and the dim proscenium of mountains. The two old ladies, of whom one was possibly not all there and the other as much all there as she was all anywhere, an unopened letter at her side, the pigeons still circling without.

"*Songe un peu, je te prie,*" rumbled Maroo.

"*Ouvre-nous des lumières!*" piped Mary Curtis.

The light was almost gone when, their entertainment concluded, Maroo stood upon the lawn to watch her friend off down the red clay road. She paused in her descent, here and there, to wave good-bye, to make certain of her direction, down and away, through the evening's dogwood, laurel, pines, dark and fragrant to define her promenade. And at last a bend in the road shut her away, and Maroo returned to her house.

The letter from Leander's college, in a hand she did not recognize, turned out to be from a young man whose name even was completely unfamiliar to her. Paul Steitler he had signed himself, and in so doing took, for the moment, a position of prominence against the panoramic background of countless other names, living and dead, that had at one time or another addressed themselves to her for reasons not, necessarily, any the less curious. She read the letter through twice, put it aside, and walked over to the piano.

Sitting on the piano bench with no back to support her, she realized that she stooped badly and must make an effort to straighten herself, and did so. She had never learned to play, had not been taught for that matter because, when she was a little girl, it had been discovered by the elderly cousins who brought her up after the death of her French father—her New England mother had died at her birth—that she did not sing well and would therefore not prove likely to succeed at any instrument. She had never learned to play, but with her long, slim fingers she was pleased to pick out melodies note by note on the cool keys of the piano she felt she might have mastered, and well, had she ever been given the opportunity. A silly tune came to her mind and with one finger she tapped it out there in the dusk. "Can she bake a cherry pie, Billy Boy, Billy Boy? Can she bake a cherry pie, Billy Boy . . ."

Keeping straight was an effort. She had not liked to walk, as did Mary Curtis, as did Tristram, so much when she was a girl as she had liked to ride horseback, her black hair gathered into a tight bun and her long skirts flapping rhythmically against the supple flank of her horse, on whom she sat easily and straight as a soldier, down shaded bridal paths in Switzerland, France, and this very South that was eventually to shelter her stoop. She had always carried with her then an atomizer filled with ammonia, and when dogs came snarling down crumbling banks to snap at the quick and nervous shanks of her horse, she would squirt it at them, sending them off yelping and smarting to regret the encounter in moist-eyed solitude.

"Can she bake a cherry pie, Billy, Billy Boy?" If only she might play the question loud enough to reach the ears of this Paul Steitler. Then, not knowing the answer herself, she might call his correct or otherwise as it pleased her. Yes, she can? No, not so much as a small pigeon pie. Then no? Oh, but why not? Why not, Billy Boy? She tinkled on the upper keys almost gaily, not gaily. He had, after all, asked *her* no question. But every letter is a great unanswered question, his no less. But he asked her only everything, and without the question-mark that makes an answer possible. She had no reason to tell him this.

He was a friend of Leander's, a clever friend, working then, perhaps, against her, her letters that would guard

Leander. It was as if he were trying to bake her grandson into a pie of treacherous understanding, of the sense of danger and the acts of fear as something more than a quaint fiction and, by his letter, to serve it up even to herself. This was a final impertinence. She would not eat.

She arose and turned on a lamp to read the letter again. He told and told well in it a little story. He had known Leander for several months now, he said, and had seen him receive letters from her, from Maroo, which he would not answer for the most part but would put aside and go on living as a boy lives at college as if nothing had happened at all. And it would have been easy to imagine that nothing had happened at all except that he never spoke of these letters; not that he went out of his way not to speak of them, but simply never did so. And, consequently, one day, he, Steitler, had asked about them and from whom they came. He had grown almost to expect a mysteriously evasive reply, but it was instead entirely straightforward— that they were from his grandmother and that Steitler could, if he wished, read one. They were not personal. And then Steitler had, would she forgive him, accepted the offer, had read not one but several, idly at first, and then with interest and enchantment.

He did not know why, exactly, he wrote, he said, unless perhaps that she might know to what extent he was guilty, and to what extent even more deeply guilty in that he could not bring himself with any sincerity to repent a sin that had for him such charm and value. She must not think him a conspirator or spy for, as Lee could confirm, his only motive in reading the letters had been one of mild curiosity. Would she, at best, forgive him in her mind if not on paper and, at worst, think him only a fool and not a sinister one? Would she, at least, accept his apologetic gratitude? He wanted her only to know something of what it had been like to enter even dishonestly and through a private gate so rich a garden.

Maroo appeared to absorb this by lamplight for whatever it might be worth to her, a cause for surprise, concern, pleasure, or yet something else. She gave evidence at least of thought as she sat there for a while without moving at all, her eyes closed and her fingertips together. If, as it was suggested, fear could be imagined as her motive, fear for Leander and his preservation, one might have thought her a little afraid then of what her admirer might show him in her letters or, more generally, more vaguely, apart from any particular person, of a sense of the possibility of complications and intensifications in the North.

And there it lay, the North, beyond the mountains, across many valleys, a difficult voyage for an old lady however compelled she might be by the sense of a situation turning in upon itself or turning only, in quickening revolutions, through a Northern sky. There was Leander, and now this friend of his and his letter. And there was Tristram Bone, who, when he had visited her not long ago, had spoken with indirection not only of her daughter Elizabeth, but, thrusting forth his great white clad arms, also of what she had surely recognized as, would she forgive him, his love.

Whatever she thought, Maroo arose presently leaving Steitler's letter on a table as unnoticed as it was to be unanswered. In that empty room, at least, there was no danger, and, outside, the mountains were placid and dark, the pigeons asleep.

C H A P T E R

IX

ALMOST from the moment they were introduced after the
lecture Motley had taken a dislike to Steitler that was to
be reinforced rather than minimized as the evening pro-
gressed. He had come close to putting his keen little eyes
out of focus looking for reasons with which to back up that
first impression and, as it evolved, he experienced no
great difficulty in finding them. The first, perhaps, was
when Steitler was discovered not to be Elizabeth's son
as Motley had, for a moment, taken him. Had he been, a
great deal might have received forgiveness. His appearance for one thing. Then his dark, heavy hair, his inquisitive eyes, the amused corners of his mouth, could have
seemed no more than a varied and coarser version of his
mother's and not the tacit declarations of a kind of contempt, as the novelist was otherwise destined to consider
them. But, instead, it had been speedily revealed to him
that the very handsome blond boy was Leander Poor, and
the other only a friend, older, cleverer, less handsome than

Elizabeth's son, and someone to be dealt with where the younger, clearly, was not.

The younger, Leander, was above all young, it seemed to him, charmingly, crashingly so, with only a slightly greater than usual grace and a deep reserve to distinguish him from any of his friends who had joined them. But Steitler, no more than six or seven years the older as Motley correctly guessed, had made use of his seniority by developing what Motley was quick to recognize as a definite *way* with him, a generally constant manner under cover—or in easy despite—of which he met the world, was recognized always as quite uniquely himself. Of just what this consisted Motley was not yet certain, but already, by the time they had made themselves comfortable by the side of the lake, sitting on outspread blankets and drinking from any number of bottles, all of which had been somehow provided them by Leander's friends, he was well on his way towards a working definition. It appeared, chiefly perhaps, to partake of a certain fluency, colloquial ease. Not only in the way Steitler spoke, though it was applicable enough there—he spoke slowly, not drawing out the words themselves but placing them at intervals from one another, controlling the silences between sentences and after thoughts, giving the impression of thinking ahead but not to the sacrifice of either what he was saying at the moment or the ease with which it was, if he so chose, possible to talk with him—for it seemed to hold equally true, this fluency, this colloquial ease, this particular control, in other matters as well. He would look at you deeply during the occasional silences, knowingly, as Motley put it to himself, as though taking a good many disagreeable, hidden things for granted. And yet Elizabeth, or any number of Steitler's other friends, might have suggested that this was Motley's impression only, perhaps, because he in reality did have a certain number of disagreeable, hidden things about him to be taken for granted and that, for themselves, Steitler's deep looks held in them no more than a kind of tenderness as though observing only so much as one would choose and be pleased to have observed. At all events, there *were* the looks and the gestures of movement as well as of expression. On their walk down to the lake, for instance, they had stopped momentarily beneath a lighted dormitory window from which some chamber music was being loudly broadcast, and Steitler had smiled his misty smile and put out his hand in an expansive, caressing, controlling arc of appreciation before starting again on his way. And above all, this way, this manner, as Motley at this early point perceived it, was distinctly Steitler's and of a tendency to color and control whatever its momentary context. Above all, too, despite its very definite style, one suspected it of nothing in particular. Where it did not charm with its half-tones, it merely passed unnoticed without giving any offense, and at the moment it seemed clearly to charm. Everyone, that is, except, of course, Motley. This was not *his* way. It offended *him*.

As underlining and giving savor to this sense of offense, Motley could not help noticing, in addition to all the flavorsome rest, the approval with which Steitler was being received by Elizabeth. Motley's curiously limited courtship of her, initiated not altogether successfully by his confidence about Bone and Bone's difficulties in the chapel the day before, and the emotions that gave spirit to that courtship, could only suffer at the sight of Elizabeth sitting beside her son's friend and being so plainly delighted with him. Motley's own demands of her were no greater than those he made of any other attractive woman of his acquaintance. Submitting by any quantity of indirect means the half-humorous proposition that even the possibility of a physical relationship was of undeniable grotesqueness, he asked only that he be granted, with this understanding, a very specialized intimacy, a brand of sympathy amounting almost to complicity. With this he could adorn himself in the critical eye of his public, his friends and, whence the *emotion* in such a courtship, of himself. That was all he asked, indeed all he wanted, but he wanted it sufficiently to make him think of his dealings with Elizabeth as a seduction and, consequently, of Steitler as a rival. Contrarily, Motley did not consider himself as his friend Tristram's rival because Tristram's demands, successful or not, would not conflict with his, whereas Steitler's did, or at least might. He could not be sure. But certainly they did at this moment, this lovely, dark, young moment by the artificial lake under the warm night sky.

The evening had not yet solidified into small groups or couples and everyone was still talking generally to everyone else.

"A bird," said one of the boys, pouring from a thermos into each newly emptied glass something that had been mixed earlier in his room, "can't fly on one wing as any rummy can tell you." And such, more or less, was the case. They were all still trying their wings with ends but not the means of their flight in mind.

"However," said Motley, "any show-off can."

"Can fly on one wing?" queried someone.

"Or walk on one leg, or see through one eye, or twitch down a road without one particle of artistic restraint. I give," he continued, breaking quickly in upon himself, "a yearly prize to the *best* show-off, and you've no idea how I've had to lower my standards."

To at least the younger members of his present audience Motley was still the visiting celebrity, and an amused silence attended his remarks. He curled his legs about him appreciatively.

"You mean parlor tricks or something?" asked Hope.

"No, no. I mean real show-offs. You know."

They didn't, of course, know, nor could they for the moment guess.

"Then whatever *do* you mean, George?" inquired Elizabeth.

"By a show-off? Well," he appeared to think, "anyone who's had something cut off or bent so he'll stand out in a

crowd. Anyone who, as long as there's someone around to
see him, will walk all doubled up with his hands jerking
out or a fancy buckle in his knee or worse. They're the
people who never know when to stop, never give up. But
come on, you all know what show-offs are!" His voice
climbed, then descended. "Hey, hey, it's a vast organization, they're everywhere, they must have a training camp
somewhere, anything for a laugh you know, a show-off
will do absolutely and positively *anything* for a laugh, and
of course ever since I offered my prize I've been simply
besieged! They hear I'm going to be at such and such a
place at such and such a time and, sure enough, there they
are, one of them or maybe even a matched pair, cavorting
around for all they're worth not knowing that the ones
who're going to win are the ones who'll put a little restraint
into their act because except in rare cases I don't *want*
anything cut off, just slightly *off kilter*, a little bit *askew*. I
ask for so little," he pleaded, "just a little restraint, and
a little originality, something just slightly unusual. *Ça
va sans dire*, I say to myself, but you can't imagine what
I get, what *tours de force*, what extraordinary tricks involving all the appendages. Why it's a wonder to me there
are any baskets left for vegetables! And it all comes down
to their definitely not knowing where to stop. But then,
once in a while you get your reward. Once in a weary while
there'll come along a talented one and oh they make it all
seem worth the trouble. Yours if not theirs."

"You know what he's talking about?!" screamed a

large, blonde girl who gave signs of having imbibed more
heavily or less artfully than the others, her face a thrill of
incredulity and triumphant hilarity. "Cripples! Show-offs
are cripples! Oh Mr. *Motley!*"

They had all sat as though stunned through his long
speech, and this outburst served as a signal for their general release, which consisted, for the most part, of laughter
either somewhat too wild as in the case of the large, blonde
girl and Steitler, or not sufficiently so as with Elizabeth.
The general result proved, however, to be the solidifying
agent they seemed to have been awaiting, for it became
suddenly possible, almost necessary, for each to locate
himself on one side or the other of the concept of show-offs
as it had been expounded to them by Motley, and they
tended, after more questioning and laughter, to pair off
in relation to the mixed nature of that hilarity. This was
not, Motley admitted to himself, just what he had anticipated. He had held forth on this subject, an old one for
him that he had not thought of for some time, because it
had seemed necessary to hold forth on something, and the
more striking the better, with which to counter Steitler's
paler manner and his apparent success with Elizabeth.
But, as with his story of Tristram at the Cloisters, it
appeared to him now that he could control these things
only so far, that he could never be sure as to their extensions. He saw this as one of the differences between himself
and his rival.

The large, blonde girl who had discovered the truth

about show-offs and seemed still by her too frequent laughter and the extreme mobility of her vaguely protruding eyes to be unnerved by the discovery, slid over to Motley and engaged him in a conversation of literary overtones. Her own unpublished, unfinished, mostly unsatisfactory novel was scarcely worthy of his attention, she suggested, but her eagerness to learn, she blinked rapidly at him, perhaps might be, and would he mind—taking a busman's holiday that is, talking shop? She had with such enthusiasm heard his exciting lecture about symbols, the stories that can be worked toward any end and then, of course, his more recent theory. She interrupted her laughter only to ask unsuccessfully for a little quiet from those nearby, the noise of whose chatter made conversation and even her laughter almost inaudible. Motley saw this as a possible device and suggested that they join Mrs. Poor and Paul Steitler who sat a little apart and would give them the sympathy necessary for their talk.

He had not wanted to venture there unequipped with bait for Steitler, and in the person of his sizeable young companion, who identified herself with a kind of archness, during the reintroductions, as Beverly, he felt that he had something of more active worth than that. One false step and the young instructor for all his fluency and control would sink into that great, blonde trap without a murmur.

"There seems to be this bottle," Steitler said by way of invitation once they were settled. This was part of his manner as Motley saw it: the colloquial expression used not only for what it was worth in itself, but for what it was worth coming consciously from him. Everyone accepted.

"Elizabeth, my dear," said Motley, touching his nose with his glass, "here's to you."

"Down the old rat-hole," said Beverly, drinking deeply of hers while Elizabeth spoke of how lovely it was to be there by the lake.

"Mrs. Poor likes things nice," Steitler explained to them.

"I really do, you know," she continued. "I lost something here once long ago—a little pair of gold dice a boy named Denny something-or-other gave me. We looked and looked but they had just disappeared off the face of the earth and Denny was even more upset about it than I. He was a *real* show-off. A lot of us were out on that island once," she pointed to a small strip of land in the middle of the lake, "drinking much more than we should have, and he got *mad* at somebody, I don't think me, and said he was jolly well going to walk home. And you know, he *did?* Walked right off under the water so that you could just see his straw hat moving slowly across the surface!" She laughed. In the interval during which their heads had been turned to see the little island of which she spoke, Steitler, who had not turned, put his hand on her shoulder and, as though he had been about to whisper something, kissed her where the dark hair was brushed back from her temple. She had no time to look at him before the others, who had seen nothing, turned back again and resumed the conversation which, still alive as she was from Steitler's sudden gesture and the mechanism of possibilities it had almost hurt into action, she felt should have been changed by it into something different and new.

"Those were the days," sighed Beverly, "and now what do we have?" She cast her eyes in Motley's direction, "but *your* kind of show-offs!" Motley wrinkled his face up into the silent caricature of a guffaw.

"You started a real Thing with that, Mr. Motley," said Steitler, "and there's no telling where it will stop." Motley, who knew there wasn't, forced a smile. "We're most of us show-offs I suppose," Steitler went on.

"Oh. How so?" asked Motley.

"Just because most of us make such a mess of keeping straight is all. A few beautiful people like those princelings over there," he gestured towards Lee and his friends, "and their young ladies," he smilingly indicated Beverly, "manage for a time." The silence he would have permitted here was interrupted by Motley, who saw his chance.

"Until they lose their little gold dice."

"No," answered Steitler. "They just forget about them, as you notice Elizabeth hasn't."

"I imagine falling in love makes them forget," suggested Beverly, returning his smile.

"Oh I don't think so," he replied, giving her his full attention, "and I suppose it's because people who are in love strike me as being the safest people of all, the very farthest from the possibility of forgetting anything, from the vaguest possibility of getting to be, for as long as they want to go on, anything like Mr. Motley's show-offs. It strikes me that when you're in love, and maybe only then, you're heading true-north, are really going straight." His silence was this time uninterrupted except by the noise of the other groups.

". . . and he makes the strangest noises!" cried one of the boys, grunting "hmp, hmp, hmp" in imitation. The others took this up. "Hmp, hmp, hmp."

"That's poor, lovely Freddy," sighed a voice like Hope's. There was more laughter.

"I don't know," continued Steitler, still more to Beverly than to anyone else, "but 'normal' is the bad word I keep wanting to use. Lovers are so unsick, and that's not the romantic notion it sounds because after all a romantic glories in the sickness of love as a long, sweet disease. Lovers don't get hurt while it lasts, and they don't forget because, like elephants, they're bigger and better than most anybody else and can see farther and last longer. And like elephants," he made his words blunt and short almost sullenly, "nobody can hurt them very much." It had been almost as though he were pouting so that when he smiled it seemed a very special gift, and it was Beverly who caught it.

"But they can hurt each other," said Elizabeth. Steitler looked at her for the first time since their encounter and smiled.

"Not very much though, or so much it doesn't matter.

The big love and the big hurt get felt so deep you can't really tell them apart."

"And it's all part of the fun anyway," suggested Motley.

"It's irregardless," corrected Steitler, lighting Elizabeth's cigarette. The flare from the match followed by the darkness only faintly broken by the half-moon made each feel in his way that they were speaking as they would not have spoken in the daytime or a lighted room. And each felt, too, the effect of the liquor not yet deadening but heightening every susceptibility into a kind of excitement. As was very often the case, it fell to Elizabeth to express these feelings recognized but unarticulated by the others, and she did so, through the soft smoke of her cigarette, to Motley. They had shifted positions somewhat so that she was nearer to him now than to Steitler and Beverly and was able to put her hand on his sleeve as she told him how glad she was to be here and that she wouldn't, after all, have thought to make the trip then except for his suggestion. And she went further, to confide in him the extent to which she was aware of how much they had had to drink there and the complicity of their picture post-card surroundings. She did not mention what had passed so quickly between herself and Paul because it became momentarily possible for her to think of that either as though it had not happened at all, or as though she had already confided it out of importance to George. That neither of these was strictly true, she also knew, but either might as well have been. As for its actually having happened at all, she had no very convincing proof; there was Steitler carrying on an intent conversation with the girl Motley had brought to them, and not even looking occasionally in her direction. And as for having confided in Motley, she had come close to that at least, had at least wanted somehow to reward him with such a confidence. But then, of course, it *had* happened. Steitler's conversation with Beverly seemed in a way as much meant for her, Elizabeth, as his earlier words about love had been, and she *hadn't*, at last, really told Motley anything. Nor had she heard what he was saying to her while she thought thus, and with exaggerated re-attention listened as he repeated it.

"I say your son seems to be making out very well with the ballet-slipper girl, but let it pass, let it pass." She looked towards them. Lee lay on the ground, his chin in his hands, his head profiled against the sky, looking slightly up at Hope, who sat with her slim legs beneath her in front of him. The others lay scattered around them, their talk lower now so that Elizabeth could hear none of the conversation. The new dimensions any continued observation of her son might give to what seemed a new richness and excitement in her dealings with his friend were more than she cared to accept so that she turned abruptly back to Motley. He was very amusing, very sheltering. She laughed.

"Well, what did you do then?" Lee asked. There was a rather long silence before Hope answered.

"I just didn't like him I guess."

"But when he tried to kiss you, what did you do?" She smiled, looking down at his chin.

"Fancy! You're a very curious boy."

"You were just about to tell me."

"I know, but then I thought I shouldn't. Oh well," she touched his nose with her finger, "if you *must* know, I burped."

Leander Poor rolled over on his back and laughed. "So that's how you show you disapprove!"

"I have other ways," she confided. He looked up at her again from where he lay, seeing her face upside down so that the little chin looked like a nose, and the mouth all turned about. He laughed some more.

"How?"

"Well, for instance. When somebody I disapprove of drops something, I step on it." She spoke with a kind of trailing vagueness, seeming never quite to end a sentence. "I give a fishy stare and step on it." They were silent again for a time during which Leander with infinite care laid his hand in hers.

"I don't know *where* my young man can be," she said finally. Lee looked up at her questioningly. "But it doesn't really matter," she concluded. "I'd never burp at you, I don't think."

"Hey thanks," he answered.

"You know what?"

"No. What?"

"I wouldn't because."

"Because why?"

"Because you're beautiful."

Lee flushed. "Oh go on."

"Silly!" she said, and laughed at him.

After a while Motley, picking these two out as the most attractive pair he could see, left Elizabeth surrounded by a group eager to tell her about the curious boy named Freddy, and joined them. Steitler, to all appearances, had swallowed the bait provided him, had sunk into the trap, and Elizabeth had seemed to pay him no particular attention anyway. He could afford now, himself, to play the game and to let it not be imagined that his particular charms were to be had any more cheaply than anyone else's. What was more, he wanted actively to join Leander Poor and the girl with ballet slippers if only that he might watch at closer range the tricks of the moon on their young faces and eyes, their hair, Leander's blond and heavy, the girl's light brown and falling loosely about her neck. There was little enough of that in his life. Oh to be young, he thought to himself, almost said out loud to himself, wistfully and sonorously, tragically, gaily, hysterically, in turn, always consciously. He was little George Motley out on a tear, and he was prepared to make the most of it. And, as almost always, he was also prepared to provide the entertainment.

They loved it, he could tell. He smiled and pouted and laughed his silent, tortured laugh or his panting, loud one, as seemed best each time, and was occasionally very grave

too, telling them that oh it was a life of drudgery he led, a
dreary bore this writing business. He shrugged his shoulders and stretched out his hands horizontally to either
side. A dreary, dreary bore. And then he smiled his shyest
smile that they might know he had made a kind of joke,
clasped his hands into a tight, pink little bundle on his
tweed lap, and talked some more. It was all going so well,
in fact, that when the large, blonde girl whom he had left
for Steitler came sliding over to him for the second time he
almost burst into tears. Did Leander and Hope know her?
Certainly they did. Everyone knew Beverly. And how was
the novel coming? "Oh well," she said intimately, giving
the elder novelist the full benefit of her handsome smile,
"oh well, that's a little something I'm going to torture Mr.
M. with." Torture? Nonsense. But where was Paul Steitler,
the interesting young man who liked to hear himself talk
about love? Gone? Oh? Oh. Gone with Mrs. Poor. He
managed a great freckled smile embracing them all. She
had become tired, would see him the next day.

"What do you say, laddy? Too much for the old squaw?"
said Motley. Leander's indifference blossomed into genuine
dislike.

"It begins, sort of, in a turkish bath," said Beverly,
laying her hand heavily upon his sleeve. In between chap-
ters he glanced about among the reclining couples, but the
girl was right, they had left together without even so much
as, could he forgive them, saying good-bye. As his annoyance grew, the deadening sense of a certain failure, there

grew with it a rather new feeling of ardent loyalty to Tristram.

In the parlance of the streets, he thought, Elizabeth was his, belonged to Tristram, though by what right he could not for the moment say. Nothing, he was correctly certain, had ever passed between them in the vaguest terms to leave such a bond or understanding in its wake, and yet it was as though he remembered an ancient and mostly forgotten law that read almost illegibly now: to each his need. This was, among other things, a law of succession saying who was to be king, and, with Elizabeth as queen, it appeared to him that the title should fall naturally to Tristram Bone, whose need was greatest, whose need was as great even as his physical dimensions which might almost, Motley thought, be its metaphor. In his mind's eye, a wider, more ingenuous eye than the one he winked from time to time at his young companions, Motley saw Tristram huge and gray as he had entered the chapel the day before as if for his coronation. There had been no Alleluia chorus, no peer to rise and uncover as the prince, the Prince of Whales, passed by not, as it evolved, to receive the holy oil, the crown, the regally affectionate hand of the consort, but to meet a crazy saint, a show-off saint who reached out a hollow stump and forced him to his knees. There had been only the indistinct benediction of an organ somewhere below, and only he, Motley, concealed in a choir stall, to watch the clumsy ceremony, the flustered and premature departure of the prince, the late arrival of the queen. And he had told of what he witnessed, who could have resisted it, but only up to a point, no mention made of the final, kneeling indignity. To each his need. Steitler needed nothing, everything prostrated itself almost wantonly within his reach, and he had only to make his slow and easy choice. He had, Motley considered, the queen's beautiful son, the real heir, and that should have been sufficient. It was Tristram's need that carried legal weight and his, Motley's, behind it. Motley's sense of loyalty expanded with his annoyance, the recognition of the betrayal of *his* needs, and his sense of righteous indignation was thus piqued from two sides. In short, they had gone, Elizabeth and the young pretender. This was wrong on Tristram's count and on his. He shut his mind's eye slowly and glared with the other at Beverly, at Leander, at Hope.

C H A P T E R

X

BEVERLY'S report was correct. Elizabeth, once she had
found herself alone with Steitler, had announced that she
was tired with the long day and the long drive, and the
young instructor had of course offered to see her back to
the inn where she was staying. And she had accepted. The
conversation was as brief and uncomplicated as that, freed
from whatever implications the memory of their earlier
encounter might have added to it. Motley had seemed so
engrossed with Leander, and Hope and all the others so
engrossed with each other except for Beverly, who had
broken away for a moment to empty the remains of several
bottles into one larger one, that they had told only her of
their departure. Elizabeth experienced a moment of guilt,
sensing that she should at least have said good-bye to
Motley because she owed him that much and also because,
for an instant, it occurred to her that he might be really
angry at her neglect, and the thought of his possible anger

was strangely disturbing. And there was Lee . . . but then there was an awareness of Steitler at her side, and it became impossible for the moment to think of anything but his presence and what had passed between them. They walked along the shore of the lake for a short distance and then up a path into the woods towards the campus. The stars were gone, the moon only faintly visible through the clouds now, and they walked through the almost complete darkness in silence, Steitler taking her hand to lead a way among the trees.

When they reached the campus it seemed deserted. Only here and there among the neo-gothic buildings was there a lighted window, the sound of a voice, a shout or, in the distance, the noise of lonely footsteps on a stone path. A low-hanging magnolia tree loomed like ghosts before them, smelling thickly sweet in the dull air, and towers were almost invisible against the sky. Elizabeth wondered at the infrequently lighted windows as they passed, wondered whether their occupants, the tall and probably handsome young men who lived in those high rooms, were reading through books with whose titles even she was unfamiliar, or whether they were talking so quietly and earnestly that no sound reached her, or making love perhaps with their young bodies in the dim light or in the dark with girls whose whispers were so faint as not to reach the open night at all. The dark windows were numberless, the stillness complicated, and only the warm pressure of his hand reminded her of Paul Steitler.

"How far," she said finally, "is the inn?" Her voice sounded more hushed than she had intended.

"A good bit still," he answered. "Tired?"

"Not really." This was, she thought, a simple, easy language.

"Would you like a night-cap? I live just up those steps." He pointed to a low stone building surrounding a quad-rangle elevated a little from the others. She stopped, thought for a moment, and assented.

His rooms were a continuation of the sweet, dark laby-rinth outside, with only one small lamp to break the night and the leaves of a tree pressing thick against a portion of the living-room window. She could not help thinking, as the young man disappeared into the other room for ice, of the earlier evening at Tristram's apartment, also lit by only one lamp and with something of the same vague sense of anticipation in the dark air. Tristram had stood about picking up letters, arranging things, as though preparing with some difficulty just the situation he wanted. With a strong sense of almost the stage background, he always, she thought, prepared the context for any interview or en-counter whenever possible, took people to particular places or met them there depending upon what was to be said or not to be, like a great stage manager deficient only in his control of the actors. He had wanted to speak to her that evening of his "crush" on her, the word seemed es-pecially accurate, and she had realized that, but had re-plied lightly, perhaps too lightly. His scenes were too complicated, too immense for her taste, and in the expression "crush" she felt implications of compression and suffocation to an extent sufficient to have made her turn idly to the letter she had insisted upon reading aloud throughout his conversation. His conversation about what? Some unfathomable story about a king or queen, suitors, revenge, and transformation, and recollections of an aquarium and a tank of tropical fish. She had only half listened, it was too much, too rich, too involved. He had seemed to want, lacking at that hour a real aquarium to take her to, to bring her by an indirect and verbal route to stand beside him and watch through the conjured glass an ugly death. Again it was the particular scene, the particular background that he sought.

It occurred to her that she kept forgetting Steitler, perhaps because his existence was so new to her, and only the sounds he made preparing their drink recalled him. If he, too, prepared the context it was with such infinitely greater ease as to make the fact almost imperceptible or, if perceived, almost sinister in its subtlety. She remembered his having said that evening that she "liked things nice" and, smiling, knew this true. What she did not know was that in addition to liking things nice she infallibly, by her presence alone, tended to make them so. Where Tristram struggled with actuality, where Steitler easily guided it perhaps, she ruled it more strongly than either of them. There was something in her manner as an attractive, graceful woman with no more than her charm needed to make her significant, that precluded the possibility of any situations but the ones in which she might move effortlessly and without pain. Steitler, returning with a tray, entered one of these.

"I'm sorry," he said slowly, seated beside her on the couch, "that I had to make love to you this evening." It seemed not so much an apology as a trailing question, and, not knowing what to reply, Elizabeth only smiled. "I didn't think you minded," he continued. There was a silence, and she knew that it was for her to speak.

"I don't know really, whether I did or not; it was lovely there by the lake. You're the second person who has made love to me in the last two days and that's more than I'm used to."

"Is Mr. Motley, the celebrated novelist, the other?"

"Oh no." She smiled at the thought. "No. As a matter of fact it was a very, very fat gentleman who keeps a monkey, so you're in good company." She expected him to make some reply, but he said nothing. The burden of talk kept falling to her and made her heart beat faster.

"You have a lovely place here." He smiled as though discounting the remark. The silences did not seem to bother him, so she tried not to let them bother her but looked out at the dark window, and the leaves against it, conscious of her profile as it must appear to him. She felt his glance and closed her eyes for a moment as though he had touched her. Instead he arose and drew an album of records from the table behind them.

"Do you like *Rosenkavalier?*" Elizabeth had no ear for music and little knowledge of it and wondered whether or not to admit her ignorance of this opera.

"I don't remember it at all."

"Well, this is the last part, the love duet, and then the entrance of the old princess, the *Marschallin*, who sees the young couple embracing as she enters. Then the elderly courtier on whose arm she leans says to her as they stand on the threshold looking in, '*Sind halt a'so die jungen Leut'* ' —'That is the way they are, young people'—and she sings out in a low, soft voice, '*Ja, ja*' and everybody's heart breaks in two."

"I'll probably weep when I hear it."

"I almost always do. Strauss never put it in stronger terms than these. This is the duet now."

As the rich music started, and then the voices of the lovers, Steitler returned to his seat beside Elizabeth. Their eyes met, and he smiled. She did not know when music had pleased her so sincerely, for as a rule she avoided any sustained exposure to it as carefully as possible. The extravagant orchestra and the high, gentle voices healing through it, seemed so strangely suited to the surroundings, the dim room, the warm and cloudy night without, and to Steitler himself, his head back under the weight of it all, that even her own pleasure seemed scarcely unusual. She sat perfectly still. Steitler, without leaning forward or looking at her, put his hand upon hers where it lay beside him, and spoke.

"Can you hear what they're singing?" She shook her head.

"*Ist ein Traum,*" he whispered to the music, "*kann nicht wirklich sein, dass wir zwei beieinander sein.*"

"What does that mean?" She looked at him, not moving her hand.

"You won't believe me probably, but it means, 'It is a dream,' " he drew in his breath as if in the effort of remembering, " 'it cannot be real, that we two are together.' "

"I believe you," she said, and believed him actually, without reserve, with curious suddenness. "I believe you." He looked at her steadily, she returned his glance for the first time without self-consciousness, and then he leaned forward and kissed her on her slightly parted lips. The hand that would, for a moment, have pushed him from her, rose instead to his face and brushed his cheek so that she could feel the tiny pricks of beard that grew there. She closed her eyes and felt his mouth hot as a wound upon hers, wondered vaguely, wildly, if it was her heart or his that rocked against her breast. There was a brief mechanical whirring as the phonograph flipped down another record and started playing it. He drew back for an instant, his lean face flushed, the hair damp on his forehead.

"I don't know what to believe," she whispered.

"*Ja, ja,*" he almost imperceptibly echoed the low notes of the old *Marschallin* as she received him again. In the quiet fury of their embrace there was something, for her, of the way in which, when a girl of twelve or thirteen walking home through the summer rain in a new dress, she had splattered it by stepping into a puddle accidentally at first and then, replacing her vanity with its opposite, on purpose, triumphantly, again and again, until her entire body was covered and alive with the new, dark splendor it wore. Home she had gone running, her brown eyes fierce and shy like an animal's, avoiding her mother, Maroo, who had not seen her, and up to her bedroom where she slipped in an instant out of the stained dress to stand naked and insane with new excitement before a long mirror. Her young body was still slim and straight, her breasts half-formed and firm, only a mist of light brown hair between her tanned thighs, and she had thrown herself onto the starched white coverlet of her bed, her knees up, her hair dark and tangled against the pillow, and caressed her own smooth warmth until, in a sudden assault of panic and fatigue, she had drawn the coverlet over her and fallen asleep with the sweet smell of cut grass filling the room.

Through the small window now above Steitler's bed the thick fragrance of the magnolia was blown and with it the first timid drops of the spring rain. They were cool upon her like a fine spray and, awaking, she sought solace in the warm pressure of his body, his mouth searching her face until it found her eyelid, her hair, her opened lips. From the living-room the phonograph played the same, last record again and again, and again and again the *Marsch-*

allin cried out her answer to the old courtier on whose arm she leaned. "*Sind halt a'so die jungen Leut'. Ja, ja. Ja, ja.*" With a quick spurt the rain grew harder, increasing in volume until it seemed that it could come no more wildly, then more wildly still, and then gently, languorously again. His breath coming more evenly now, Steitler whispered something to her so softly as to be lost in the sound of the slow rain and the music, and Elizabeth replied with the tiny, muffled laugh of a girl.

CHAPTER

XI

I⊤ was not until early in the afternoon that Steitler
stepped out into the gray, cool day. The rain continued to
fall slowly like a heavy mist, coating the stone walks with
a dimly shining dampness and making the dense green of
the grass and trees seem denser and greener still. To keep
himself dry he carried unfurled above him a large plum-
colored umbrella with a tear in it that had been left behind
by someone once and had since become moderately famous
among his students. It was Sunday, and there was little
activity on the campus. Only here and there did he meet a
boy hurrying somewhere in a hat crushed out of shape by
everything but wear, or a couple straggling towards the
railway station, the girl with a kerchief tied under her
chin, the young man looking unconcerned with the weight
of her suitcase, a damp cigarette between his lips, her
hand limply in his. Steitler nodded to some of these, dip-
ping his umbrella slightly, and not recognizing any of them
for the most part, but imagining at one point that he saw

133

Hope of the evening before skipping along without a kerchief well in advance of the young man who appeared to be carrying her bag. He called out to her, but she did not hear him.

After a cup of bad coffee alone in his room he had gone out more for the sake simply of going out than with any particular goal in mind. The rain neither enticed nor repelled, but only trickled down his big umbrella off onto the upturned collar of his old army-officer jacket as he walked down the path. Hope, if it was Hope, had not heard him, and the chances of their ever meeting again were as slight as they were unimportant to him. Perhaps Lee would invite her down one day. Leander Poor, freshman, member of the varsity crew, grandson of Maroo, son of Elizabeth. He was perhaps the very last in a long line of people whom Steitler at this time did not, for an equally long line of reasons, want to see, but, half perversely, half idly, he turned his steps in the direction of his friend's room.

The boy had just awakened and was lying sprawled out under a light blanket when Steitler entered. His face was still flushed and his blond hair dishevelled from sleep, but his eyes were bright and awake as they took in the dark figure before him.

"That crazy parasol of yours!" Steitler smiled, collapsed it gingerly, and leaned it up against the door he had closed behind him.

"Don't you rise when a professor enters your room, Poor?" he asked.

"I would have," he answered, "would have snapped right to it the moment you came in, but I'm always full of lust when I first wake up, and I was afraid if I did it might show."

"Don't then," said the young instructor, brushing a pair of white socks and some khaki trousers off a deep-seated arm-chair and sinking down into it.

"O.K." Lee replied, closing his eyes as though he considered going back to sleep again. Steitler gazed out of the open window and watched a bird trying to pull a worm out of the wet earth like an illustration for a child's primer. The sky was mottled gray, and the rain continued to seep down from it.

"Where are the others?" he asked finally.

"Beats me. We were all out pretty late—except you and Mother." He sat up against his pillow.

"We were pretty late ourselves, went back to the room for a night-cap and played a lot of records."

"You don't say. Then she's probably just getting up too."

"Did I wake you?"

"Oh no. Somebody shoved a letter through the door and I heard that. Must have come yesterday. By the way, where is it?"

Steitler leaned forward and found it under the clothes he had brushed to the floor.

"From your grandmother."

"Maroo." Lee jumped out of his bed and stood naked

in the center of the room. Thrusting out his long arms as far as they would reach, he stretched his tall, well-built body, tanned around the surprisingly white loins at other times protected by his rowing shorts, and yawned.

"Maroo, Maroo, Maroo."

"Anybody," said Steitler, his hands on his knees, "with a name like Leander Poor should by all rights have looked more like a gnarled show-off than a Greek godling."

"Oh go on," Lee answered, brushing the hair from his forehead. "Let's have a look at it—the letter." He sat down on the floor, his knees flopping out like a fakir's, tore open the envelope, and started reading. Steitler glanced up at the wall above him. On it hung a large red and black banner, seven or eight champagne corks strung together like beads, and the photograph of a group of young men standing about in semi-circle holding long oars like lances at their sides.

"She says," Leander spoke without looking up from the letter, "that it's warm in North Carolina, that Lydia Dorn sprained her ankle trying to climb out of a downstairs window when she saw Cora somebody-or-other coming up the driveway just at lunchtime, that Miss Curtis is coming to read French with her in the afternoon, and that the sun is making," he squinted at the small round script, "a burning-glass of her spectacles and so she will have to stop. Well, what do you know?" He looked up at Steitler with a broad smile.

"May I see it?"

"Sure."

Steitler crouched down beside Lee, putting his hand on the boy's bare shoulder to steady himself as he read.

"Here, let's sit over here, it'll be less complicated," Lee suggested and dived back to his bed where he stretched himself out on top of the covers. Steitler seated himself at the foot, Maroo's letter on his lap, and resumed his reading.

"Incidentally, Paul," said Lee before he had finished, "did you ever write her as you said you would?"

"Just like I said," Steitler looked up almost peevishly, "I wrote her."

"And will she answer?"

Before Steitler had a chance to reply, there was a crash that made them both jump. Lee tore the blanket off and tried to wrap his nakedness in it; Steitler merely sat still where he was, his head spinning from the noise. The big plum-colored umbrella which he had left leaning against the door had of course fallen with a slam to the floor when the door opened. On the threshold, a light pink coat buttoned up to her chin, her hair misted from the rain, and smiling, stood Elizabeth.

"The alarm sounds. I hope I haven't interrupted anything. Good morning."

As he repeated her salutation with his lips, rising from the bed, shaking her hand quite in the manner of someone who had only just met her the day before, as was indeed the case, Steitler's eyes in silence greeted her physical

presence questioningly, fearfully, as though expecting to
see some extravagant, deep-colored change wrought there
by their earlier intimacy, merely by the heat of his body,
his mouth, against hers if nothing else, or the cool spray
of the night's rain. Only when his eyes at last met her
own—she was talking to Lee, who had ducked behind the
closet door to dress, and Steitler was thus able to look
longer and more searchingly than would have been otherwise possible—was he reassured that for her what had
happened had simply happened. She was prepared, the
situation already falling gracefully into place about her, to
consider it, incredibly enough he thought, as no more than
that. In two cases alone, it seemed to him, would such a
reaction be possible: either with a woman for whom a
night spent with a strange young man was in no way re-
markable or out of the ordinary, or with one of such
exquisite breeding, such a delicate sense of distinctions, as
to render the fact by its very uniqueness no more than a
curious accident and a matter for lovely indifference. Almost, he continued in his mind, it would need the daughter
of Maroo, whose letter lay white on the floor between them
where it had fallen like a tiny handkerchief. Illogically,
he wanted to retrieve it and with a cavalier gesture present
it to her with his compliments, then a gay invitation
phrased in the dim, soft words that had been part of their
language only a few hours earlier.

She smiled at him, at his long glance, and in more
startling terms than ever before he confronted the awe-

some possibility of falling painfully and intricately in love with her. For the first time since he had stepped from his rooms into the slow rain he felt fully awake and alive, and the new consciousness involved new questions. Why had he come to Lee's room, who and what was Lee, and why their friendship? As the boy emerged from his closet, fully dressed except for a necktie that he tied before a mirror as he continued talking to his mother enthusiastically about nothing in particular, Steitler made his answer. Lee was, after all, Lee, the invulnerable, safe, brilliantly handsome young man whom, along with less than a handful of others, Steitler had befriended in the fervent, insane hope of acquiring through some mysterious channel a particle at least of that invulnerability. He was not in love with the boy's mother, nor could he manage to feel now the danger of the possibility. She proved herself, even as he looked at her, as much out of his price range as was her mother, who would of course not answer his letter, and perhaps even her son. But this recognition did not prevent in Steitler a richness of affection for the three of them, and it became possible for him to look at Elizabeth as she took off her coat and brushed the dampness from her hair, as something of such worth and beauty that even the impossibility of having her as his for longer than the few, dark hours the night before, thieved him of none of his delight.

"And so," she continued, widening her conversation to include both Lee and his friend, "it's just a matter of collecting George and driving back to the city. He'd gone out prowling somewhere when I got downstairs, but I left him your room number, Lee, and a note telling him to meet us here."

"I hope he enjoyed himself," offered Steitler, "with his lecture and the lake and all. At least he didn't get mixed up with Beaver Smyth and his bride."

"Oh, the one who introduced him," Elizabeth laughed. "I think he had a good time, at least I hope he did. I feel a little badly about having left him all by himself last night but I *was* tired."

"Oh, he got on all right," put in Lee. "He had old Beverly wondering what hit her."

"Which reminds me somehow, Elizabeth," interrupted Steitler, "of your glasses I broke. Why don't you leave them here and let me have them fixed. It was only the lenses wasn't it?"

"Nonsense," she replied, "I'll have them fixed myself, the better to see you with, my dear, both of you, though you," she indicated her son, "wouldn't bear much closer inspection. Do at least wash your face like a lamb."

Lee was on the point of leaving the room for this purpose when Motley appeared in the door bundled up as though for a hurricane.

"Speak of the devil, what?" he said, his sharp eye glistening damply from beneath his sou'wester. "Like a bad penny is young George." He unclipped his yellow oilskins and tossed them over the bed-post. They all greeted him profusely, even Leander whose dislike had abated if only out of respect for the novelist's valiant powers of survival in the face of Beverly and all those bottles. He took a seat on top of the desk and wiped the drops of rain and perspiration from his freckled forehead.

"Well, you left me in the lurch all right, my dears," he said to Elizabeth and Steitler without looking at them, "but I managed to have a clever time of it anyway and this morning has been," he looked to the ceiling for his adjective, "divoon as a young lady said to me yesterday." There was just a little more or less than humor in his reproach, and Elizabeth was quick to catch it.

"I felt so badly about running off that way, George, but I was so silly and all-in and you seemed to be so involved with everybody."

"Don't mention it, dear girl, the Motleys are justly notorious for their radiant dispositions and to me it made no nevermind at all. Though I might have added," he went on, making the most of it, "that for anyone as fagged as you, and you *were* tired, I could tell, you stayed out rather late. Imagine my surprise and concern when, after breakfast at a respectable hour, I inquired for you at the desk only to discover from the cretin in attendance there that you had returned with the sun as he put it. I thought at first he meant *your* son, but he insisted upon the star, the glorious, life-giving."

"I'm afraid it was my fault," broke in Steitler, "we listened to *Rosenkavalier* from beginning to end and it was raining and all."

"And you're a pill anyway, George, for asking questions that might be more difficult to answer than they are," added Elizabeth.

"I ask nothing," he insisted, "nothing except that you allow me to say a few words on the subject of all that I've managed to see this morning in this fantastic place." And he proceeded to tell them of his travels through the campus. With his quick step, aiming his small feet at the pavement like missiles, he had inspected the entire area in the space of the few hours allowed him. Gothic library and gymnasium had given way to Romanesque auditorium, these to Ionic temple athletic office and Georgian dormitories, to a mansard-roofed something-or-other, and Motley had stood for a few minutes in the rain before each of them, feeling the damp muzzles of stone lions, peering up at the heavy, bird-stained features of late trustees and presidents, and decided that the easiest and most judicious attitude to assume towards Elizabeth would be one of poignant forgiveness. It was not as if he weren't annoyed to have been abandoned to the enthusiasms of his young companions, deserted, in a word, a distasteful one, by her and the youthful instructor whose disfigurement he contemplated with each leaf of ivy he twitched off walls as he passed them, but simply that to act disagreeably would have been to gain nothing. His wrath was never heroic, he knew, and to stamp his wet little foot would have been, like Rumpelstiltskin, only to watch with dismay as it splintered through the floor, trapping him there, and making it necessary to ask for the aid of sympathetic hands that might free him. Instead, let him merely give Elizabeth his magnanimous smile, Steitler his indifference, so that she would know that with him anything went so long as she granted him, with equal understanding, his simple requests; so that Steitler would know that his little triumphs were a matter of staggering unconcern to him, Motley.

As soon as he reached this decision, however, he had meditated, nodding absently to the greetings of two members of the English department on their way to chapel, upon just what he would be soon forgiving Elizabeth. Her neglect, of course, and her disloyalty to their mutual friend Tristram Bone, but perhaps—perhaps more than that. Her extremely late return to the inn took place long after he had pulled the blanket over his ears to drown out the racket of the heavy rain, and he was consequently not present to search out some memento in her expression of what might have taken place during the long, dark hours of his sleep. Probably nothing, probably no more than a sustained conversation dominated throughout by Steitler, which would have undoubtedly enraged him by its style if not its subject, and to which he could have added a good deal had he been there, and probably, he guessed correctly, some music, some good whiskey, some rot. And then, without very much more thought on this matter, he had found Elizabeth's note, gone to Lee's room, and come upon the three of them established there.

In little more than an instant, for he had extraordinary perceptions and suspicions in such matters, he was convinced that there had been more to Elizabeth's escapade than conversation and music. How much more he could not be certain, but it occurred to him, despite his dislike for the young man, that there would be no particular grotesqueness in a physical relationship between Steitler and Elizabeth. In any such admittedly impossible relationship between himself and her, as between Tristram and the saint, he thought, the grotesque would unavoidably prevail, but to imagine the young instructor as having made love however passionately the night before would be to imagine no more than the vaguely incredible. And, for Motley, this very incredibility only made the assumption the more plausible. He was as certain as he needed to be. There had been, without a reasonable doubt, considerably more to Elizabeth's escapade than conversation and music.

He could not have explained this conviction, though he would have been pleased to try, but there was a languor, or a tension, or a kind of triumphing propriety, in the air that was as excitingly unmistakable to him as the scent of raw meat to a hungry puppy. He changed his plan completely, twitted Elizabeth on her desertion, her late hours even, postponed his projected forgiveness with zest, and only when he saw that it was all being taken too seriously, as seriously as it was given, offered his smile and went off into the description of his tour. Even as he spoke, his thoughts turned to the richness of the discovery, the exhilaration rather than the anger occasioned in him by it, the exultation, the delight. This was a little something straight from Heaven, from who knew where, to him, to him alone for the moment at least.

". . . and it's been really divoon," he continued, "being here, meeting you all," he clapped his hands together at his own enthusiasm, "and how sad to have to leave it all behind. Elizabeth, my dear, will you drive me, will you whisk me off through the dark and dangerous day in your shiny automobile with me singing Strauss to you all the way, back to the old grindstone and I don't mean T. Bone?" There was valiance in the way his eyes met theirs, Steitler's, Elizabeth's, Leander's.

C H A P T E R
XII

MONDAY morning found Emma Plaut busily at work waist
deep in the clear sunlight that spread in through a window
whose upper panes were shielded from the day by a venetian blind. The room was a small one where Bone was in
the habit of dressing, and one door, now closed, led into
his bedroom while the other, by which Emma had entered,
opened on a darker hall. All his clothes hung there behind
the sliding doors of a long closet built into the wall, his
linen filled two tall dressers on either side of the window,
but there was evidence that he used the room more frequently than its special function would seem to imply.
There were an old leather couch with seats so low that
they almost touched the floor under human weight, beside
it a small table with a pile of books, a lamp, a copper
ashtray upon it and, hung around the dark green walls in
white frames, a dozen or so large Audubon prints of birds.
Lying open upon the couch was a bulky package of his

laundry, which Emma was in the process of piling neatly in drawers, and, over the back of a straight chair, his evening clothes, which she had in mind to brush off and hang away in the closet. She was working quietly and swiftly so as not to awake her employer, who, she imagined, lay asleep behind the closed door.

She had not been told, nor had she yet discovered, where he had gone the night before. The breast pocket of his dinner jacket had revealed no theater stubs, and that eliminated her first conjecture. Always, she knew, when he went to the theater, the stubs found their way into the breast pocket of his dinner jacket, and there were, this morning, plainly enough, none there. *Und so.* It made no matter. Probably he had gone only to dinner somewhere, and this could be ascertained in any number of ways later. At least she knew that he had stayed late over his eating because it was now almost ten, and he had not yet come out for his breakfast. She picked up an armful of shirts and laid them on top of one of the dressers preparatory to arranging them in the drawer. She had not been unaware of the presence of the monkey who sat still on the table worrying the fur on his little pinched chest, and glanced over at him now to see him turn his bright eyes upon her expectantly.

"One of these for you maybe?" she said, the air thick with her question, holding up one of Bone's shirts for him to see. She tore off the blue paper band that bound it and

let the linen fall to its full length. Its immensity made her
chuckle, and the monkey gibbered, waving his hands out to
the side.

"For *der Knochen*," she referred to their master in a low
voice by the German translation of his name, "they are
just right, but for you," she held the collar up under her
chin, "and for me, they are too, too *gross*." She laughed
again. The sleeves hung down almost a foot past her ruddy
hands, and she could have wrapped the white cloth around
her thin waist twice. "For you, for me, *ungeheuerlich gross*,
but for him, no. So." She folded it deftly and placed it in
the drawer with the others. From its frame above the
dresser a great white pelican looked beadily down its
swollen yellow beak at her. The monkey showed his teeth
and returned to the fur on his chest.

When she had finished with the laundry, Emma turned
to the evening clothes, which she hung from the top of the
hall door, caressing the satin lapels as she brought her
hands down and then starting to brush them vigorously.
When it was put away and the sliding doors closed, she
crushed the laundry paper into a large bundle, thrust it
into a waste-paper basket, and started to straighten up
the room itself. In order to arrange the books into a neater
pile it was necessary to disturb the monkey, which she did
by lifting him up under the arms and placing him on the
floor gently, sympathetically, because she bore him no
grudge this bright morning. She even tickled the top of his
head between the thin, protruding ears as she turned from

him, and with this encouragement he scampered across the floor, leaped to the door-knob of the hall door and swung back and forth from it holding on by one hand and squeaking excitedly. She put her finger to her lips and shook her head slowly from right to left to quiet him, but though his eyes grew wider and his swinging more hesitant he only mimicked her gesture and continued his chatter.

"He sleeps heavy," she muttered, "but not that much, so off, off!" She fluttered her dust-cloth at him and, after snatching out at it several times, he dropped noiselessly to the floor and stalked to the corner, his fingers trailing the carpet, where he crouched in silence.

"Be good boy," she warned, and returned to the books one of which, by revealing itself as a volume of Goethe's letters, renewed unpleasant memories and took its place at the bottom of the pile. She was wiping out the ashtray and straightening the lampshade when the bedroom door opened and her employer entered.

He wore an enormous dressing-gown of deepest red brocade with a braided sash whose thick tassels reached almost to his slippered feet. His face was still closed and heavy-lidded from sleep, and his gray-brown hair lay in a few loose spirals on his forehead, about his ears, and over the back of his high, broad collar. He stood in the doorway for a moment without speaking, adjusting himself to the sunlight, this newest moment, and the presence of his two witnesses. Without realizing the glazed intensity of his stare, he searched Emma's careful face as though to discover there something of what the day might become for him. She stiffened slightly, and the faint change in her expression was sufficient to complete his awakening. He bade her a warm good-morning, which was returned respectfully, then went over to the monkey and jiggled the tassel of his sash before him.

"Diddely, diddely, diddely doo," he said in a tiny voice as the animal complained to him. "Rimbeldy, pimpkin, flibbedy jib," he added as an afterthought, and the three of them smiled. He preceded Emma majestically through the hall and into the dining-room, where he took his place at the table as she raised the blind that he might have light by which to read his paper.

She was hesitant about initiating any conversation because she preferred for the most part to leave to him the burden of turning the key in the queer lock of a new day, and because one of the rules she remembered most clearly from her girlhood was that gentlemen frequently do not choose to converse upon any subject at all when newly arisen. She went so far as to smile efficiently as she removed his orange juice glass and replaced it with a cup of black coffee and a plate of buttered toast, but no farther. He returned her smile, she noticed, but only to return in an instant to his paper.

She could not help but regard this morning's taciturnity with a twinge of regret because the mornings were otherwise full of his most unguarded moments. They involved, for instance, the wearing of the one garment in all his wardrobe that seemed to glorify rather than to restrain his enormity or, as she put it to herself, to suit him. The others were of gray or dark blue, of cool brown or, at best, of expansive white, but this, his dressing-gown, was of richest red, and she rejoiced in it. He became for her a great cardinal, a *Herr Baron*, a celebrated *Kavalier*, when he wore it, ready to grant from the folds of its magnanimity any number of petitions, any quantity of confidences. And this morning he only sat quietly enveloped in its richness, one hand bearing the ceremonious weight of his chin, the other extended white upon the soft mahogany, while he looked down as if from a great height at the printed page before him. Hoping for the best, she allowed a cube of ice to fall with a tinkle from the silver pitcher from which she filled his water glass. He looked up.

"Would you see who's at the door, Emma?"

"It's not the door, Mr. Bone," she replied, and was about to explain that it was the ice when, to her confusion, the doorbell rang in the kitchen. It was too complicated and sad to explain. She disappeared into the hallway.

She liked Mr. Motley—had, on a number of occasions, enjoyed the opportunity of opening the door for him, and was pleased to see him standing before her now, his heather-green hat in his hand. He was a real gentleman.

"Good morning, Mr. Motley," she said.

"*Guten Morgen* to you, Emma," he answered with a gay smile. "Is the great man in?"

"Mr. Bone is eating breakfast." He often referred to

him as the great man, and she liked this. "Got up late."

"So I see," he glanced at his watch to confirm it. "Better late than never! I'll find him."

From the living-room where she deposited his hat she could hear the rumble of Bone's greeting, the lighter accents of his friend's reply, a pause, laughter, their voices again, but no single word. To reenter the dining-room now had something of the thrill for her of walking across a stage even though there were no lines to be remembered. Emma had, of course, never walked across a stage in her life, but she had entered the dining-room a hundred hundred times, and still it was able to excite her somewhat. Neither of them broke the conversation to give her any notice, but Motley thanked her when she brought him a cup of coffee. The monkey had crept in and was enjoying a seat across from his master. She retired to the kitchen, and the little animal alone was left to observe the two men.

Motley was speaking with interest and animation to his friend and the restlessness of his hand, which, unlike Bone's, would not lie still on the table, snared the monkey's attention. One by one the fingers rose and dropped with tiny ticks of their nails to the shiny surface, then the whole hand squirmed sideways, flattening itself out as though crushed, and then the fingers again, dropping one by one, inching forward like little blotched worms. The bright eyes of the monkey followed each movement however slight, and slowly, unseen by anyone, he started to slide his paw towards the scuttling white thing. A report of laughter startled him, and he withdrew it in an instant and bobbed up and down in his chair in an agony of excitement.

"Yes, that is my project," Motley continued, folding his hands before him. "A tragedy about homosexuals, they're enjoying such a vogue now, but a tragedy mind you. And the recognition scene will take place, I think, in a urinal. I'll have a fan to blow the sick smell of that pink disinfectant they use into the theater, and there will be startling chords done somehow—not music of course—as the eyes meet. It would go terribly well, you know. The crazy situation in dreams where, one by one, each of the good, friendly people, the guides, unmasks and reveals himself a hideously smiling member of the hysterical conspiracy. And finally there will be only one left, this one and my hero, and then they meet and it happens, and the chords. And in the urinal, mind you, the urinal!" He paused and the momentum carried his hand out onto the table again where it twitched itself into a fist. "I'll tell you how it starts too. A couple of actors, the hero and another perhaps, will come slowly to the front of the stage, face the audience, and start screaming, screaming so loud the veins stand out through their greasepaint, so that ears split in the first row, and then they will stop, go back into the set and, when the walls stop ringing, start the action. The screams will be the overture, the prologue, maybe even the chorus and, yes! the epilogue too, only at the end perhaps just the hero will come out—perhaps not to scream this time but just to give a long, low whistle or, no! better still, I'll have people planted in the audience to scream and then—curtain!" He paused, leaned back in his chair, and looked at Tristram.

"Did you mention this in your lecture Saturday?" Bone's face was immobile, tragic.

"Oh no." Motley suddenly sounded tired.

"How *was* the lecture by the way?"

"Not bad, not bad." Motley brightened. "But it was the weekend itself you should have seen, Tristram. What a time was had!" Bone touched a napkin to his lips and raised his eyebrows. "There was Lee Poor and of course Elizabeth, and this young fellow named Paul something-or-other, Steitler I believe, and after my talk we all went down to a lake with blankets and bottles and about half a dozen undergraduates and their dates, and there we all stayed and stayed until it was absolutely imperative that we go to bed, singly or in pairs. I," he let his shoulders sag mournfully, "singly . . ."

"Who is this Steitler? A friend of yours?"

"No, no. Of Lee's. A young instructor in the English department who went with the Poors to hear me and then down to the lake with the rest of us. I think the phrase is, 'a very charming young man,' rather good-looking, glib in a way, and quite successful with the ladies, pip pip, God bless 'em," he raised his coffee cup to eye level and then took a sip from it. Smacking his lips, he put it down and continued. "In the privacy of the boudoir, however, I will confess to you that I took a scorching dislike to him. There was something outstandingly contrived about him, not quite sinister but almost. Would you mind, by the way," he interrupted himself, "asking that spy of yours to remove his unholy eye from my person?" He indicated the monkey who had crawled to the table and sat there as if transfixed by the agile novelist.

"Here, here, my lad, you're unnerving us with your innocent eye," Bone reached out a brocaded arm and gathered the animal to his lap. "Rest yourself, be serene, it's a troubled world, surely, but in the name of God it must be kept as long as possible from the children. Don't you want to grow up to be like Mr. Motley and myself? Well then, lulla, lulla, lullaby-loo." He shielded the monkey with the folds of his dressing-gown. "You were saying?"

"Thank you. That I d, i, d, n, apostrophe, t, like him."

"Who?"

"Steitler. Paul Steitler."

"That was uncharitable of you, George."

"Uncharitable, my ulcer! Then it was charitable of him, I daresay, to monopolize all conversations and run off with Elizabeth into the bargain?"

"Under the circumstances perhaps. It might have been."

"Really, Tristram, you are a source of unceasing amazement to earnest George. Just like the midget there. What's his name?"

"Since he is pleased to remember none of them, I find it convenient to have several. You could call him Galahad, the pure in heart."

"Or even Tristram."

"If you like."

"Well, no matter. I was merely suggesting that if charity should begin at home, then the distinct lack of it should end there. It's of you that I was thinking."

Emma came in to see if they wanted more coffee but, upon sensing a kind of tightness in the sunny air, decided against interrupting them. She removed a bowl of fruit from the sideboard instead and retreated with it again to the kitchen.

"You're being distressingly vague and ominous about all this," said Tristram, not waiting until the door had swung closed behind her.

"Oh I'm a fool," answered Motley, and for a moment he seemed to believe it, "a real fool. They went off and left me that evening, you see, left me with a big blonde who wanted to talk about writing, and we talked all right, until I could hardly see straight. I could almost have wept, damn her, and so I was annoyed with them of course. Then, the next morning, I wasn't; in fact I'm not now exactly. I don't really know why I came to see you today. Except that I do know." The sun shone full on Bone's face so that his blue-green eyes seemed incredibly light and transparent as they regarded the new look of sincerity in his friend's shadowed expression.

Motley, finally, after countless inner revisions of his own position in the situation, relayed to Bone the full extent of his suspicions concerning Elizabeth and Paul Steitler. Even when he had concluded, when he looked across the breakfast table to his friend to see what *he* would say, he wondered what form the story had taken, what color or shape had emerged foremost from all the words he had barely heard himself using. As it happened, Bone said little. He had risen from his chair, setting the monkey down on the floor to run out into the living-room, and had walked over to the window whence the sun on his dressing-gown seeded red lights in all the silver, the glass, and polished furniture. He had said nothing for a few minutes, looking out into the day with his back turned to the novelist, who sat with only a certain uneasiness to obstruct the rich sense of relief at having done, for better or for worse, what he had come to do. Motley was not certain himself as to why he had done it, why he had told his tale. He was seldom certain at such times and alternately either cursed the looseness of his tongue or the sensitivity that made him overly aware of it. To Tristram he had given as his reason for the telling a desire to keep the record straight, to have everything set down somewhere (the reason, perhaps, why he was a novelist, he suggested), and this was probably a good half of it. The other half was what caused his uneasiness, that and whatever might be Tristram's as yet unexpressed thoughts on it. What motive would Tristram assign to his having suggested, his having come on purpose to suggest, that Elizabeth, his Elizabeth, was having an affair with a young man named Steitler? Furthermore, what indeed *had* been his motives, Motley wondered. But then, Tristram had allowed him little enough time for such conjectures since in a moment he turned from the window and faced him.

His expression had been as bland and clear as the day without. He wiped a crumb from his chin, and then replaced the white handkerchief in his sleeve. The sun streaming in from behind him almost blinded Motley, who had turned around in his chair and squinted up at the great head that seemed as if suspended in the morning haze before him. Then Bone had spoken. His voice was low and undisturbed, but the words were distinct enough for Emma to be able to hear from the kitchen albeit she paid them little attention on the whole, scarcely noted them as of even momentary importance within the conversation. He merely suggested that Motley's peculiar gifts tended to make him animate and inflate whatever might seem to him the most appealing among the host of potentialities attending any unextraordinary human situation; that if, as certainly *might* be the case, there were validity in his suspicions, he, Tristram, could be no more than very interested to hear of it. The entire question of whom one loved, he continued, Emma looking up from her work for the first time as she listened, seemed to him of relative unimportance. It was whether one loved at all, and how much that love cost, and what was its reception then, that mattered. He raised his eyebrows and smiled.

Motley saw far enough into the very ease with which his friend spoke to bethink himself of sunning waters and queer winds, of his heather-green hat in the living-room, and of a luncheon engagement with the important critic, Whitewall, who would talk from behind his gray moustache, through a mouth no bigger than a dime, of the politico-moral responsibilities of the artist—a curiously reassuring, dispensable set of responsibilities, he thought, compared to those involved in his remaining any longer with Tristram Bone. And soon the little novelist puffed a quivering smoke ring through the air, rose to his feet and thought out loud about having to make his departure. To hell with Whitewall, but then—the critics. One understood. When he had written his tragedy at least he would have a different set of them to worry about. That was a comfort. And it must be a comfort to Tristram not to have to worry about making *his* living. There was something, he supposed, for everybody. He pushed open the kitchen door and shouted through the pantry to Emma. *Aufwiedersehn! Danke schön* for the coffee. *Ja, ja*, Mr. Motley, *ja, ja*. By the time she had reached the dining-room they had already gone into the hall. Bone accompanied him to the door. They would meet soon. They shook hands with greater than usual warmth, and Motley, taking in the sight of the huge red figure once more, made his farewells, cocked his hat over one eye, and clicked the door shut behind him.

It all happened as quickly as that, and while Motley sank down the long, dark shaft in his elevator, Tristram leaned his forehead against the closed door for a moment and tried to remember just what had been said. Then he went into the living-room and sat down at the writing desk, aware of Emma who dusted nearby, and only with difficulty breaking away from his prolonged meditation of an enigmatic ink stain on the blotter before him as he answered her.

"You were out late last night, Mr. Bone?"

Yes. It had been late. His eyes that had glistened superbly as he spoke to Motley in the sunlight dulled here in the comparative gloom of the long room whose deep purple carpet absorbed what little light there was.

Who but himself had listened to the conversation in the dining-room, had even so much as seen what transpired there? Not Emma, who had sat two rooms away, catching an occasional phrase only to discard it as humdrum; not the monkey, whom he had held in his lap shielded by his dressing-gown from what went on; not even Motley, who was prevented from hearing what he said by the sound of his own voice as he said it, from seeing what hung about him by the bright haze in which it was suspended. Tristram had heard and seen everything, but he seemed not well to remember it now as he slumped in his chair with one hand on the telephone, his eye back on the ink stain.

Emma gave a little cough as if from the dust she had carefully removed from the shoulder-high candlesticks on either side of the fireplace the day before. The monkey's head pivoted towards her from where he crouched in the little chair with its pattern of dark rosebuds near his master. Bone lifted the receiver and dialed Elizabeth's number with his finger.

She was in. Would she drive off with him for the afternoon? Did she remember that letter of his she had read the other evening? They would, if she liked, go to the booby-hatch mentioned therein. Good. How was Leander? That did not surprise him. Splendid then, he would come for her after lunch. She would be ready. He replaced the receiver.

"Will you be back for dinner, Mr. Bone?"

"Very likely." Three fat wrinkles strained on the back of his neck as he turned towards her.

"It will be beautiful in the country on a day like this!" she exclaimed, forgetting the candlesticks.

"Yes. Why don't you take the afternoon off yourself and go to the park?"

Emma returned to her dusting, the line between her colorless eyebrows deepening. "Maybe," she said. "Maybe I will."

Tristram looked down at the monkey, then picked up the telephone again.

C H A P T E R
XIII

A YOUNG man of twenty-five or so, wearing overalls and carrying an empty bucket, pushed open the wide, green doors of the aviary to be greeted by a gust of piercing whistles, trills, chirps and murmurings from the double row of cages that lined two walls of the long, low building. He stood on the threshold for a minute as if reconsidering both the necessity and the risk of entering, then beckoned to the girl who stood slightly behind him, and walked in.

Sunlight seeped thick and golden through the high, oblong windows above the cages and fell in broad shafts to the linoleum floor where he dropped his bucket. A cloud of dust arose from the impact, to be gilded into a thinner mist as it drifted upwards in a slow diagonal. The girl coughed in the semblance of irritability. She was younger than he by a few years and wore a faded blue dress rich in contrast to her ash-blond hair pinned into tight curls. Drawing herself up by her hands, she took a seat on top of a large grain chest. The young man was handsome in spite of a heavy stubble of beard and the incomplete set of teeth that his grin revealed to her as he attached a long hose to the faucet and started washing down the floor. They did not speak, but the birds seemed disturbed simply by their presence and the sound of the water, and continued to voice their excitement as they flitted about behind the wire. Their cages were of different sizes, varying from small ones that held no more than a bird apiece through larger ones with many occupants to one great one that dwarfed the others. Each opened through a small door at the back into the partitioned flight enclosures which ran along the building on the outside, and these doors were mostly open now, permitting the birds to hop in and out of the daylight at will. Though they did not speak, the silence between the young man and the girl was clearly more involved with their contemplation of each other than of the birds whose still, incurious eyes belied the frantic measures of their cacophonous trills and varied, flittering wings. She watched him work, turn off the water and start sweeping it down past the cages, and, only when he glanced up from time to time, looked down at her pink nails, which she cleaned idly with the end of a pin. The grain chest on which she sat contained a number of drawers each marked by a white card with its contents spelled out upon it— millet, hemp, canary, sunflower, teasle, rape, thistle, poppy, sesame—and when the young man finished the cleaning, leaned the broom in a corner, and disconnected the hose, he came over to it with a number of small tin troughs on a tray which he set down beside her. At the brush of his hand against her as he put down the tray, she slid over to the other end of the chest. He reached out and pushed her gently on the shoulder, and then opened the drawer between her calves. She drew her legs up beneath her, closed her eyes and looked away in mock contempt. He filled the troughs and started down the long room placing one in each cage.

The room became more filled with birds than before as they flew and hopped in from the flight enclosures to beat their wings in the air above the seed and screech out at the gluttony of their competitors. The girl jumped to the floor, picked up one end of the hose that lay uncoiled nearby, and played with it slowly as the man went about his feeding. She twisted it into a knot, let the water left in it trickle out into her palm which she shook and dried off on her dress, untied it, and made it wiggle like a snake on the linoleum. She spoke for the first time then and called down to the far end of the room to ask when he would be done. He looked up at her as though she had broken a rule but grinned as he told her soon, as soon as she'd leave off fiddling with the hose and give him a hand with the seed. She smiled in spite of herself, but continued toying with the rubber tube on the floor.

Putting down his tray, he walked over, took up the other end of the hose, and gave it a gentle tug. She did not relinquish her hold, but gave it a flip that made it squirm in his brown hand. He tugged again, more boldly this time, and with a short, defiant laugh. She did not flip it again, but merely held it tight in her fist. The game was established by this, and, charging at her with his eyes down the length of rubber between them, he swung it so that her entire arm was obliged to follow its wide, skip-rope motion. She responded with no movement of her own, but met his eyes with a kind of flushed, half smiling persistence and continued to resist the little jerks he gave to wrench it from her.

When this had gone on some few minutes enriched by the chattering of the neglected birds, he gave one more unsuccessful tug and then, making sure that she was watching him, took a length of it and let it fall limply from his other hand which he pressed tightly between his loins. She gave a little exclamation of disgust and dropped her end. Leaving the hose quiet in the sunlight, he came over to her, took her face in his large hand, held it towards him so firmly that her mouth was all puckered up like a fish's, pressed his wet lips to it, and kept them there in spite of her fists with which she pounded his shoulders weakly. With his other hand he pressed her body so hard against his own that she gave a little grunt and pushed his face away. He released her. She whispered fiercely.

Fat boy would be coming soon, they better hadn't. Fat boy would be driving in soon, from the city, sure, so let him just, then—. Well, she wouldn't. Honest, but she, breathing sweet, hard, *couldn't*, what with fat boy and them birds all squawking to be fed: them finches, macaws, mynahs, swallows, and the mash to hurry to them: spiders, strawberries, paprika—live meal worms, boiled eggs, molasses, sticky, thick, oh sweet! She touched consolingly his warm excitement, and queerly then forgot the willful game of skip-hose in the musty, bright-floored bird-house, with the sun all blond as she was, spilling in on where they sat, lay, there against the grain-chest, worrying—about them birds! Hose the birds! But, see, you couldn't. He was loony to suggest it, switch his long, lithe hose into them, her all flustered to behold the flying feathers, greet the fat boy maybe or, at least, her sweetheart's father who'd be back soon to take over, show the place off to its owner who'd be there soon, from the city! He had money and positions. Hose the money, fun the other! Loony! Laughter. O.K. then, but later. Dumb-eyed came her answer: maybe. O.K. but, for Christ's sake would she, if they *was* to wait a little, leave off, let him put it where it came from? So she let him, and arose then as he brushed the seed-dust off him, coiled the hose up in the corner, started once more with his feeding.

The African gray parrot shrieked at the crushed banana thrust before him, but ate it nevertheless, his ancient eyes bright to either side, indifferent as to the young man burning on past him in the sunlight to the next cage. Before a flight of waxbills, manikins, and cardinals, the girl stooped to fix the cuttlebone that had fallen in the wet moss which, with her sticky fingers, through the wire, she worried to retrieve the white, bill-whetting hardness, and to escape the direct notice if possible of the young man's father who had vibrated up the dusty road in his pick-up truck and stood now on the threshold, peering in to see if all was finished, ready. Was his boy to make a barn-dance of it, girls and all, the job scarce started? Well, let her help him if she could then, no hard feelings. He'd best in and change his shirt. Just pep it up a little, would they now?

Whatever could be done through the thick fragrance clinging to them both, of molasses, the mash, their desire, they proceeded, with scared fingers, to do, until the crush of heavy tires on the gravel roused the father from his shaving, sent him to the window out of which he yelled to them that he, that they, was here, right now, and to go out and tell 'em howdy for him while he finished. The girl only stared with increased concentration at the tri-colored nuns she was busy with, and the young man alone arose and went valiantly to receive the big man in whose employ he and his father were.

Tristram helped Elizabeth out of the car and guided her across the lawn, through the vegetables, to the aviary.

"That will be one of the boobies now," he whispered to her, indicating the young man with bad teeth who approached them.

"Tristram, what is it *really!*" Instead of answering, he shook the young man's hand, remembered his name miraculously, and introduced him to Elizabeth. His dad would be out in a jiffy—shaving he guessed, grinning. The three of them entered the building together.

Elizabeth, who was the first to enter, found herself suddenly confronted with an extravagantly complex toy arranged in long rows to either side of her, all sparkling and
scarlet, brilliant white and noisy green, intricately mobile,
and piping, crooning to her in the slow sun from the high
windows above their heads. She did not, even, at first,
notice the figure with the small, blond head done up in
tight curls that stooped by one of the nearer cages, nor did
she respond adequately to the shy greeting the girl offered
when summoned to them by their young guide. This, then,
was Tristram's booby-hatch, a division of his leisure of
which she had somehow never heard, and these, then, were
the boobies—not the young couple with the kind of complicity between, but the birds. The birds continued to
entrance her. A sulphur-crested cockatoo winked its black,
unseeing eye at her, fire-finches flitted crimson among the
damp leaves of their sanctuary, and almost at her elbow
ice-cream-pink cocks-of-the-rock with their puff-ball
combs and ivory talons screeched disinterestedly from
their supple perches. Bone permitted her fascination until
the brisk arrival of the Mr. Carter or whatever it was, she
did not quite hear, who managed the collection for its
patrons, a handful of city gentlemen of whom Mr. Bone,
by virtue of his superior interest and generosity, was chief.
After an exchange of pleasantries, he led them down the
long room, the girl hanging back, the young man accompanying them in grinning silence, stopping here and
there before particular cages, pointing out, among other

phenomena, a canary who did four *"tours"*— *Aufzug, Glucke, Schnetter,* and *Zitzit*—sang four different measures, and its mate who had already mastered two of her own— hollow roll and water roll—in addition to the original flute. Birds were usually happy in cages, he continued, his long face flushed with his eloquence, and you could tell easy when they weren't, and their reasons too: bullied by another bird, for instance, or having trouble with the mate—his wink included them all—or sick maybe. Some were bound to get sick, and then they didn't sing, would mope, refuse to eat and even die maybe. There wasn't, if the expression could be pardoned, one hell of a lot to do in such a case. Did Mrs. Poor know, he wondered, that wild birds never died natural deaths but lived in continual danger and always, except in aviaries, came to accidental ends? His son put in a few jests of his own, gestured towards scarlet teen-agers, patriotic buntings, fly-by-nights, and double-breasted seersuckers. His father caught the spirit of this and added in an undertone to Bone the name of the zippered nutcracker whose cry, this would kill him, was "ouch!"

It was a glittering tour, with the low tones of their human voices only occasionally drowned out, like last mutterings from a death-bed, by the shrill ornithological solicitations, and Elizabeth found herself quite ready to pause when they reached the largest cage at the end of the room. It was concerning this that Tristram legislated, as in the letter Elizabeth had once read, that there be no bars, alarms or barriers of any kind to obstruct the freedom of its occupants. Behind the wire, which served only to keep them from filling the building itself, hopped, flew, chirped, murmured, or were silent, sparrows, pigeons, bluejays, whippoorwills, and all the birds that could be trusted to wing at will through the open door at the back, to return or not as it should please them. Tristram looked at her as Mr. Carter explained the special emphasis here, and she showed to him by a smile her recognition. They went up the other side of the room then, until finally it was apparent that they had seen everything. The young man broke away for a moment while Bone congratulated his father, whispered to the girl who had remained by the door during their absence and, shaking hands once more with Bone and Elizabeth, said he guessed he'd shove off for a little. His father, making his guess too, suggested that Mr. Bone and his lady friend might like to draw a free breath themselves and that he'd be in the house if they wanted anything, and for them to be sure to stop in for a coke before they got ready to drive back to town again. And so it was that the two were left alone.

Tristram knew scarcely where he should begin. The drive, though a rather long one, had passed uneventfully. Elizabeth had talked on of her projected trip to the West Indies that summer with Lee perhaps, of her friends, of Ann who was going to have a baby after all these years, of poor Philip and Alice who weren't. It was only when she spoke briefly about her last weekend that Tristram's hands had tightened on the wheel, but she mentioned simply that it had brought a great deal back to her, that she had foolishly broken her lorgnette there and must remember to have it mended. For the most part her companion, who managed an occasional nod, a "yes," a "really," listened to what she said not at all, but merely to the pleasant sound her voice made as she spoke. Strangely, he had thought, she did not question him, except for an off-hand allusion to the mystery when he met her, concerning their destination. This warmed him somewhat, imagining, as he did, that she had thus not come out with him for the novelty of the surprise awaiting her, but as though to reestablish herself after whatever had happened earlier; to rest gratefully on the first great rock that rose from the limebright waters about her. And now they were here, standing among his birds, and she was tired, asked almost plaintively—the intricate richness of color and sound, the sunlight that seemed to ferment through their musty surroundings into something even thicker and more golden than itself, to oppress her—that they go out for a little into the air.

Behind the aviary lay a small apple orchard, beyond it an unmowed field stretching slightly downwards, and up this the clear afternoon breeze blew, cooling them. Bone spread out his large handkerchief beneath one of the trees, Elizabeth seated herself upon it, and he lowered himself with difficulty to the grass beside her. She had not said she was tired, but with her face profiled towards the wind, her still eyes gazing down the field and her hands quiet upon her lap, Bone felt that there was no need for her to say it, to say, perhaps, oh Tristram I am tired, tired, let me at least with you find rest, here, for a moment, in the sweet panic of this latest spring. There was no need for her to say it, he knew, watching her beside him, but nevertheless he wished it said if only that he might answer, slowly, seeing only the new leaves gesturing above them, that, yes, he knew and understood, they need speak no more but simply descend with colossal languor, like creatures under water, towards an overwhelming repose beneath the pull of any tide. But, as it was, she had said nothing, nor had he, and his recollection of all that Motley had implied that morning at breakfast would force him to speak to her at last as he had planned, to ask her somehow, though she all but cried out to be let alone, of what had happened while she was away.

Why Motley had told him, why he must ridiculously, having no rights, question her, and what she might answer were problems he had tried since his first enlightenment to thrust from him. What had already, in spite of his efforts to the contrary, started to flower into an immense despair as he dressed himself before his mirror, had abated somewhat as he left his apartment and stepped out onto the street. The city could be, for all its stony angularity, he had thought, as valiantly part of the spring as even the little apple orchard where now he sat silently beside Elizabeth, and he had looked up at the bright roofs of buildings, the partitioned sky, and down to the blinding, windy pavement, to feel, at last, that perhaps it would be possible to go on for the moment as though nothing had happened. His way to the garage had taken him through the open square at the foot of the park where, as if to confirm his growing sense of the rightness at least of *things*, he had seen once more the gilded statue of the general on his horse and the angel who held the bridle and guided them forward. Her golden arm stretched out, she pointed with a golden finger, and as usual Bone's eyes followed her direction and stopped at the bronze lady standing un-clothed in the fountain before them, in her arms a shallow bowl from which water trickled. All this was as it had always been, as it should be, and there was even a special gift as he crossed between the statues, a huge and moving point of gray between the immobility of gilt and bronze, and proceeded to the side-street that led to the garage. On the corner, waiting for a bus, had stood a young woman, and just as he was about to pass she had dropped a coin which rolled on the sidewalk before him. Without so much as breaking his stride he had managed somehow to retrieve the bit of silver, to press it into her gloved hand with a slight bow and continue down the street so gracefully and effortlessly that the very wind blew his praise. Never in all eternity could he have repeated it, but never, he felt, would that be necessary. It was only once, perfect, a unit, and it had happened in full view of the statues behind him. As he crossed to the garage there came, to augment his exultation, a sense that if everything else went wrong and failed there would still, triumphantly, be that; that all his life was perhaps a progression towards that moment and could descend now easily from it; that he had been created perhaps for no reason more obscure than that he might one day pick up that silver coin and return it to the young woman who had let it fall as he passed. His love for the young woman would live beyond death. And here now he was beside Elizabeth, the memory of this encounter rich within him to bolster and pad, but sad in that it was presently and precisely incommunicable.

"Tell me, how was George's lecture Saturday? You promised me a report," he asked.

She turned to him and there was no weariness at all in her expression. "Good heavens, I don't know and I'm sure that's terribly revealing. He went on for a good hour about something, told some jokes, spoke a good deal about plots I think, and everyone, including myself, clapped long and loud when he was done, but, to save me, I can't remember exactly what it was all about!" She looked at him in dismay.

"Well, I daresay that's more revealing about poor George than you. At any rate, he seems to have survived it."

"Oh, you've seen him?" She did not particularly mark her question for an answer, but it was, after all, the pivot-point, and Bone found himself replying—that indeed he had. He had seen George, George had drunk a cup of coffee with himself and Simon that morning, had told them of a play he planned to write, then on to the subject of his weekend, all that he had seen, a good amount of what he had thought or wanted people to think that he had thought, and to the description of a young man named Steitler.

Elizabeth only nodded recognition of the name, wondering that the apple tree did not break as Tristram leaned heavily back against it, and come crashing down green upon them, pinioning them there as in a dream, unable to rise, to move, only to speak on and on until everything was said. She saw herself in this position, bound by a branch, wreathed in leaves, with only the white face of her companion visible to her where it lay pressed to the grass, one heavy-lidded eye peering through the foliage, the great body miraculously lost somewhere in the tangled, fallen tree. There she might tell him all there was to tell, confide in him as she imagined persons condemned confided in one another, all that strained within her as she had lain as involved with the young man's body as with the tree that held them now, of how he had whispered to her through the craziest moment of their involvement that he had never known such loneness, that she was not there at all, it was a cloud he clasped. But she had been there, oh Tristram yes, there, there, but not loving, only living the young man down to where he was less than a face pressed by chance to the grass; she an old princess enjoying her last lover with the sin of an old smile, through all that

pulsing sweetness, at the child at her breast; her powdered
neck arched back over the white pillow, wearing him like
a garment upon her. Did he, did Tristram, know what it
was to have smiled, for an old queen to have smiled invisible to the last of her loves, in the dark and burned by
the faintly merciless rain, his love thick in her like the
song of birds, with nothing, nothing to say? Could he,
could Tristram, answer, though the sod had almost stopped his mouth, his eye closing like a flower closing, or
opening, under the weight of their tree, and tell her why
and how, he never having for so long, if ever, might she
be forgiven, loved. But no, no answer, none that she could
hear at least, and somehow then she freed herself, squirmed
out and stood all stained with green, her secret safe there
in the great form which she might, but would not, free
from his imprisoning apple tree. Each spring she would
perhaps return with pretty sentiment and growing old to
see what change the year had fostered, festered in that
vernal ruin, until all was bone. And so it was all said,
silently, in her imagination, as Tristram leaned back
against the firm trunk, his hair disarrayed by the wind.

When he spoke at last it was to ask her, almost as though
under the assumption that she might reply with even a
particle of what he wanted to know, what she thought
could have driven Motley to imply what he had. He
described that implication to her with a hundred indirec-
tions that it might be set apart, might become something
they could both observe as dispassionately as the leaf he

picked from a low branch and let drift to the grass before them, but for all his circumlocution the nearly precise nature of Motley's suspicions emerged brightly enough. This was unfair, of course, to Motley, and his anguish grew with the realization, but he could scarcely afford to be deterred by that; it was unfairer still to Elizabeth. Why did he say it, why with all his eloquence could he not say it even half as gracefully as he had picked up the coin, why did his words fail? But he knew that his words did not fail. It was the fact that failed; the fact of his love and of her indifference that failed in final importance as much as anything. What had it cost them to be as they were? The price he had paid at least was monstrous, and he felt the prize fall apart about him, inarticulate, beyond salvage, to be loved excessively, defensively, like a broken thing, even as he awaited her reply.

She was shaken almost to tears by her anger. Motley, who only did what he must, she could forgive, but Steitler, who had somehow betrayed her, and Tristram, who had obliged her to face that fact, would receive the full rush of her wrath. What they had done was not so much to imply her dishonor as to force her to the surface where the situation was no longer nice, no longer an easy progression and, most important of all, no longer in her control. This was unforgivable. Her mind made a wild revolution casting up so much she scarcely knew where to turn for her words. Somehow, immediately, she must silence Steitler, like a tyrant in a myth cut out his tongue and thus prevent him from confirming any part of what Motley had suspected, Bone had taken for true, any part of what had happened between them actually, fantastically as she suddenly saw it. Even as she started to speak, her voice quiet and brittle, she had no idea how this was to be done and, unable to think ahead, let herself be drawn forward by the force of her own angry words.

Quickly she lost her dim feeling for Tristram as someone left unprotected, to be treated always gently, and everything that had led her to think of him thus, his unarmed enormity, his taciturnity, the concern for her that rose in his eyes as she met them, changed into proofs of the new impression that he was a great, unassailable inquisitor hunched on the grass beside her, beyond the reach of all but her cruellest, sharpest words.

She said that the absurdity and untruth of his implications were more even than she could manage to laugh at, that if they were part of a joke it was a bad and ugly one. Without stopping to consider that Steitler had had neither the time nor the opportunity to suggest anything, she blamed him as violently as Bone and continued, curiously, to let only Motley escape. From the confusion of her revolving indignation she rescued somewhere the sense of need for an accomplice, someone to assist in her distress, and Motley, partially because she felt that he would otherwise constitute her most dangerous opponent, assumed that position in her mind. He had based his suspicions and his testimony on some malign or malignly witless word or act of Steitler's, but he could be persuaded by his noted affection for her to retract this; he could, could he not, be made to see his mistake? It was Steitler who must be silenced forcibly, struck dumb. It was from him alone that a kind of ruin could come, and as her hate and fear of him grew she softened somewhat towards Tristram, who sat motionlessly listening, and spoke recklessly on about the young instructor.

". . . that of all people you should think that I could have had an affair with him! Tristram, he's no good, he's a glib, clever schemer with I don't know what sinister something to his discredit, and he has completely dominated Lee you know—I don't dare think for what reasons." She spoke rapidly, catching out always into the millrace for a device with which to silence Steitler. "He has kept him from leading a normal, sane life with his college friends by hanging around always, a boy half his age, filling him full of his strange ideas, and you know," she rushed on, her heart beating swift at the wildness of what suddenly occurred to her, "Sunday morning I went over to Lee's room to say good-bye and can you imagine what I was confronted with! Why as I opened the door a huge umbrella that had been placed carefully up against it went crashing to the floor like a danger signal, a warning gong, and there I saw him, this Steitler, on the bed with my son, sitting there beside Lee, who was lying on his bed with nothing on, and his friend beside him. Oh really I don't know what I can do, and then to have you go on as you have, suggesting that *I'm* somehow mixed up with this person is almost more than I can bear—almost more than I can take." The intense dismay in her voice as she spoke of Tristram's cruelty stemmed more from a growing recognition of what, in her panic, she had implied about her son, her awesome accusation against Steitler, which so frighteningly involved Lee. None of this had occurred to her before, and she knew its falsity even as she phrased it, for the falling umbrella had meant nothing at the time, she could suspect no such perversion of either young man; with Lee it was absurd, with Steitler she had the memory of his love to ridicule it, but she had spoken blindly, she had devised a threat with which to slit her lover's tongue, and to have by so doing wounded her son became only another weight to the great wheel of her wordless, apprehensive rage.

She wanted suddenly, acutely, to lie down and sleep. If the apple tree had but fallen earlier to pinion them there it could all have been so easily done, she could have told everything and then either slept beneath the weight of leaves and branch, or escaped, as she had imagined it, left the little orchard, the aviary, and oh Tristram, to return uninjured. Instead, no tree had fallen, she was irrecoverably tired, felt, more strongly than even her fatigue, the disagreeableness of the situation, the aching unpleasantness of what she had created. There was the comfort of no motive to which she might return since even as her mind slowed once more she could find no reason for having spoken as she had, and only her statement itself continued to spin. She had said that Steitler was probably having an abnormal relationship with her son, and she had said it to keep him from betraying her, to make the possibility of an affair with her seem grotesquely impossible; but he had not betrayed her, he was clearly having no such relationship. What had flung the thought out into her mind, how had she been able to say it, and why? But then, at last, for all its horror, it would, as she saw it, work. It appeared to work even on Tristram because he spoke to her now with a kind of slow sadness as if to show his concern for her as hurt rather than hurting. If what she imagined were true, he said, then it was a sin, a sin heavy upon Paul Steitler. The word had no reality for her, but as he spoke it, his eyes wide and puzzled, she had at least to consider it.

For his part, Tristram had found himself concerned at so many levels that it became necessary to find some way by which he might somehow be able to speak of them all. For his own peace at least he must be accurate in what he said, and, whatever the complexity, Elizabeth could always choose the level at which she would be at greatest ease. There were so many. If she had spoken the truth, as he could not be certain, then there was the whole new situation between Steitler and Leander to consider and her own despairing part in it. If she had not, or even if she had, there must be a new adjustment made between himself and her, for it was not as if he had lost nothing by

speaking to her as he had. It was evident that in some
manner his loss was great. He shuddered almost visibly
to think how great, and indeed shuddered at more even
than that. Everything seemed to be falling apart about
him as he thought, and of all the hopeless wreckage not the
least deadening aspect was, for him, the growing, devour-
ing complications it occasioned. Who or what was first to
blame he did not know. He, in part, was at fault by having
initiated the present conversation; Elizabeth equally so,
especially if she had lied about Steitler, and Steitler himself, of course, whatever the truth of the matter. If nothing
else, he knew at least that, whoever the sinner, it was
something like sin that had set the damaged, damaging
machinery of complication in action, that both the sinner
and the innocent would suffer through the new intricacies,
and that it was in these terms alone that he might speak
as complicatedly as was necessary, despondently, merci-
lessly necessary. And so he had continued, Elizabeth
taking his words as concerning no more than Steitler and
Lee and what she had said of them, as being intended
chiefly to console herself.

"When anyone is walking his lonely tightrope," he
paused, the image growing in his mind, "without a safety-
net, with a minimum of courage or conviction and a maxi-
mum of vulnerability, dangerously, imperatively, it is a
kind of sin for someone else even to suggest that by jump-
ing down there is nothing to lose but a precarious balance
and the questionable safety of the far platform." As he

continued, Elizabeth had the uncontrollable vision of Tristram, enormous as a balloon in spangled tights, clutching a paper umbrella, and himself teetering, through the screaming light that flooded him, down a slender rope high above a circus of faces, and momentarily it was as if she must either fly off into laughter or sob until something— the rope, the tree, the dream—snapped. It was perhaps the nearest she would ever come to such madness, and in an instant it passed. She had missed part of his words.

". . . sin more deeply than this by going beyond the comparative innocence of such a suggestion and, by the flattery of his solicitous presence alone, and the danger of his affection, if we may presume its particular unnaturalness, almost flipping the younger or more innocent performer to the lower trapeze from which, with his superior acrobatics, he has probably managed thus far to swing in reasonable security. If there is a sin beyond forgiveness, a sin against the Holy Ghost, perhaps, involving the pride that admits of such arrogant interference with another soul, then it is with that sin I suspect we are concerned." She was moved by his justness, the truth of what he said, only to remember that its basis was apparently her own untruth about Steitler.

"For myself," he went on, smiling as if, to her, for the first time in an eternity, "I can only hope for forgiveness— from you, and then, again, later. I shall burn for a time, of course, how long I cannot now think, but at last, with painstaking mercy, I will be allowed perhaps to rise a little

if only because there has been so much burning—" he
looked away from her into the wind, "here. But, my dear,
we can be certain of so little. Whatever is to come of it
all, we must do only what we can, for it is a long time
coming. I am sorry for whatever I've caused you this
afternoon, sorrier than I've said, but do not blame me if
you can. With everyone always thinking, thinking, and
saying little, there is so much blaming and misunderstanding and so little kindness. Oh let us be kind!" he said, and
Elizabeth laughed with him as he reached out and patted
their apple tree. Behind her laugh spun still her anger, the
anger and fear she continued to feel for Steitler, for all
she had said in her panic. Behind Tristram's, he did not
know what. A kind of final admission, a last eloquence
perhaps, and the sudden recognition of his determination
to go one ridiculous step farther and see this Steitler, find
out from him what he could, what little he could ever find
out from anyone, about anything. And behind his laugh
too, making it ring truer than Elizabeth's, was his thought
of the birds, the birds so near him in their sanctuary, the
lovers who tended them.

CHAPTER
XIV

DESPITE the profound despair with which he viewed the present situation, Tristram Bone was able to take a kind of obscure pleasure in his note to Paul Steitler, which he composed shortly after returning with Elizabeth to the city. He was not certain as to the spelling of the young man's last name, nor could he be sure that an envelope addressed simply care of the English Department of the university would reach him, yet it was a part of his pleasure, recognizing this, to consider the possibility that the letter, whose mere creation was enough in itself to relieve and commend its author, might never perhaps be read at all. There seemed also to be a certain nobility or authenticity in the act to further what was almost his enjoyment in writing it.

He had written that he hoped, on the basis of a matter profoundly concerning them both which had come recently to his attention, that he might be forgiven the liberty he took in addressing someone who could scarcely be aware even of the fact of his existence, let alone any situation through which they might be sufficiently involved with one another to justify the interview he wrote to arrange. Without saying more of the situation than to mention the name of Elizabeth Poor as being somehow implicated in it, he proposed that Steitler come to the city and meet him, perhaps, at the Cloisters if he knew of them, had an automobile at his disposal, and was willing to make the trip on what would appear such slight provocation. They might have their talk there undisturbed by Emma or the monkey and then return for dinner at his apartment. They might meet in the hall of the unicorn tapestries, which, if he did not know them, should be sufficient inducement in themselves, and he would have no difficulty in recognizing himself, Tristram Bone, because he was, he said, stout enough seldom to escape unnoticed even when competing with medieval hangings of such splendor as those in question. It was important somehow to Bone, in the way of maintaining what articulate sanity was possible in all that had happened, to make this proposal even if it were to be lost or ignored, and he had posted it with a sense that he was doing, at least, all he could. He had suggested the Cloisters as their meeting-place not only because they would be undisturbed there, but because the scale of those surroundings tended in a sense, he thought, to justify both the immensity of his person and of all that he had in him to say. There was also an unpaid debt to the monastery involving the earlier unpleasantness in the chapel and making it neat and right that he do this kind of penance, find out from Steitler what he could, sure of being pained whatever his discovery, in full view of the ancient walls, perhaps even of the particular saint, and surely of the unicorn whose agonies would be portrayed about him. They would witness just this much more of Tristram Bone, and then he might go his way to that extent absolved.

He passed the two days during which he half awaited an answer to his note, half expected none, rather quietly. He did not see Elizabeth, though he considered telephoning her one afternoon, discarding the notion only when it seemed undeniably wiser to wait until he had either seen Steitler or it became clear that he was not to, for otherwise he would really have nothing further to say to her, nothing to add or to subtract from what he had already said. If he could somehow have managed to see her without being obliged to speak he would have done so because what could be borne with comparative ease as long as they were together became a kind of throbbing despair when they were apart, but this was, of course, not possible. And he did not see George Motley. A paragraph in his newspaper announced that the novelist would speak on a program with the critic Whitewall in one of the large lecture halls the next day, and for a time he thought of going but again decided in favor of inactivity, the seclusion of his apartment, and a few walks through the spring air as it swept bright down city streets and across the park. The only occasion he was unable to avoid was a dinner party arranged some days earlier for the purpose of paying back a number of social debts. His life of organized leisure placed him, from time to time, in such a position with people who were not among his older friends but who had entertained him for one reason or another so that they must, as he saw it, be repaid, and to assist him in this he would call upon one or two of those whom he had known longer and better. From that category, on this particular evening, he chose a Jewish doctor and his wife and one of the gentlemen who had an interest in the aviary with him. The doctor, who was not prevented by a metal brace on his paralyzed left leg from joining Bone on occasional walks as far as the natural history museum across the park, had tried valiantly some years before to discover a cause for his friend's obesity and a way to eliminate it and had been kept on despite his failure because he knew something of what it was like, Bone felt, to carry a great burden. He spoke of all men as being in one way or another cripples and in need, yet could laugh as if none of this mattered really, could see a kind of beauty in the broken, spiraled shell Bone had picked up once on some southern beach and kept, chalk white and startling, on an otherwise bare and dark table in his living room. The doctor's wife, large-busted and slow, accompanied him and was, as usual, mostly silent except for statements concerning the trials of keeping house, directed in German to Emma, who passed things among them and answered with never more than a word at a time. The bird-fancier, whose round, sallow face looked, as the doctor had once confided to Bone, like an udder, had been particularly befriended by Tristram when it was learned that he had, as a young man in college, been suspected of genuine lunacy when it was discovered that he took copious notes on everything— not merely on his courses and the books he read, but on conversations he overheard in trains, on penciled inscriptions on the walls of lavatories, the number of steps to be climbed to various places, the days he felt depressed and the days he was nothing so much as happy, and yet he made nothing of these notes, simply kept them all in a long shelf of loose-leaf binders and said that one day he might go over them and discover all that there was to discover about their author. He was somewhat younger than his host and, having gone to the same college at the same time as Elizabeth's late husband, was the only person of Bone's acquaintance who had known him. Bone himself had known Elizabeth during the elder Leander Poor's lifetime, but the marriage was short, and he had actually never met him. The bird-fancier could tell him little, but there was, he had declared, no doubt a great deal of information on the subject somewhere in his notes and as soon as they were properly indexed he would exhume it. For the time being, his only definite recollection was of a tall young man, blond, with deep-set eyes who drank a good deal, married young and well, and never returned to college reunions. The bird-fancier himself had never missed one; in all the years Bone had known him he had never indexed his notes, but there was always hope that he might. He would peer through the thick lenses of his spectacles and say that there was.

These were the friends Tristram chose to assist him with a party he did not want to give for people he scarcely knew during the interim between his note to Steitler and the possibility of an answer. There was a Russian prince, thin and with a kind of battered, bemused valiance about him, who told with zest how his sister, expatriated and impoverished, had died of hunger because she was too proud to ask her neighbor for the second time how to light her stove, and how his brother had succumbed to fatigue because there was no one left to open his bed in the evenings. Some chose to believe him, some did not, but all were amused. The widow of a celebrated sculptor who had arrived fringed in a copious red shawl, a lace bandeau about her elaborate gray head, laughed guardedly before continuing her discussion with the doctor by remarking that one could not, in translation, capture, she groped nobly for a word, the *granite quality* of someone or other, the incomparable Frenchman. She would not look at her listener as she spoke, but merely swept his face with her eyes occasionally, en route to some more distant object, another guest, or the impressive figure of their host, who was trying to keep his attention fixed on what he was being told by a woman whose name she had not caught. The woman was, as it happened, a distant relative of Bone's, but so distant that he felt justified in seeing her no more frequently than he did. She would speak, as now, largely about the family they had in common, and Tristram, as the only child of elderly parents about whom his memory was remarkably slight, tried honestly, almost desperately, to follow what she said, but could add little to it. His childhood, for all the tenderness with which he indulged his recollections of it, appeared to him no more than one long, long summer, thickly green and still, involving games that required him to find a bush or tree large enough to hide behind, and the fact that the very woman before him had from time to time, by her own admission, partaken of the cricket-droning dusk and excitement of that endless summer was a fact of which he could somehow not think clearly. Emma's announcement that dinner was ready alone saved him from telling his relation that he could scarcely remember even whether he had been generally happy or generally sad as a child, let alone any of the playmates with whom he had apparently shared that forgotten emotion. As they rose they changed the subject to Emma's faithfulness, the gradual disappearance of her sort from the face of the earth, and followed the doctor who limped ahead of them into the dining-room with the sculptor's widow much as he limped out of it again, once the meal was finished, explaining in undertones to his wide-eyed wife that the Russian prince had meant no harm, that it was only his way of being friendly, and that it scarcely mattered anyway.

The latter part of the evening was dominated by the monkey, whom Tristram cajoled into joining them that he might relieve his master of a part of his responsibility. He had dressed the animal in a diminutive dinner jacket and silk hat long ago provided him and set him on the carpet in their midst to do what he could. When Bone made the gesture of tipping an imaginary hat and said "Honor the ladies," Simon would in reality lift his and bow to whatever lady happened to capture his attention at the moment, which was the one trick they had arranged between them. The others depended upon the occasion. He would lope about the room in slow circles, seeming to parody first one guest and then the other, and so deeply did the wordless simplicity of his humor affect them that they laughed scarcely any the less delightedly when he drew one little leg stiff and hobbled over to the writing table in the manner of the doctor. Tristram drew forth the tiny purple chair, and Simon took it in his arms, sat in it, bared his teeth and gibbered, moved it, turned it about in a puzzled way, and then made gestures with one of the upturned legs so obscenely that the bird-fancier submitted the question as to whether he did all that he did out of mimicry or genuinely, out of a dark past, and with conjectures upon this they amused themselves until Bone finally, in a kind of desperation, two days having elapsed with no word from Steitler, no reassurance from Elizabeth, arose suddenly and said illogically, there being no evidence of boredom among them, that he refused to tire them any longer with the monkey and could anyone else suggest some other amusement before retiring.

The pomposity and peculiar rudeness of his interruption struck him as soon as he said it, but in a few moments several of them were on their feet exclaiming upon the lateness of the hour, the sculptor's widow told him in low tones that he must come to see her, she paused, some evening, she paused again, letting her glance rest only for an instant upon him, and have a little talk, then made her departure. So soon, in fact, were the consequences of his act to empty his apartment completely that the apprehensions concerning his discourtesy gave way to an overwhelming gratitude, and he was able to fall quickly asleep. It was the next morning that a reply from Steitler had finally come.

It was short and concise and gave no clue to the feelings of its author. He would expect to meet Mr. Bone at a certain hour at the place he had suggested. There was no more.

With the fruit of his action before him in the form of Steitler's reply, Bone had suddenly to take stock, almost to exclaim at the length to which matters had been brought. More strongly than at any time earlier it appeared to him with what reassuring conviction he had heretofore suspected that there would be no reply. Yet here it was, unfolded before him. He, Tristram, whose manner was ordinarily one of vast passivity, slow movements as though under water through space, found that twice now he had acted in earnest, had taken the independently formed situation and forced it, actively, if not to change its course, at least, for hence his most passionate motive perhaps, to proceed articulately. He had gone to Elizabeth and confronted her with Motley's suspicions, he had heard out her panicked defense, and then, most incredibly of all, carried possibly by the momentum of his interview with her alone, he had made these arrangements to see Steitler, to discover what *he* could add, and was now within a few hours of that meeting. If ever he had cried out to sink back into a kind of submarine safety, away from the giddy surface where actions, now partially his own, folded into each other like waves to heave him forward through the cold ocean wind, if ever he had prayed to redescend to where he might once more move with fluid speed and ponderous grace, it was now. What had he done?

He lay half clothed on the leather couch in his dressing-room with the rest of his mail unopened beside him while a choir three times larger than any ever before assembled screamed the question at him so thunderously that he had to put his hands to his ears to escape being deafened. He drew his monstrous white knees up and buried his face for a moment in his arms, a tremendous athlete saying his prayers before entering the arena, the room smelling faintly of the perspiration that trickled down his swelling neck and the huge, fruitless loins. Seven million cheers for the favorite who was, or was not, he, rushed through the blind in a lattice of light and dark across his bare and mountainous back.

There was a tiny, microscopic silence in the long hall where the unicorn tapestries were hung. Six of them there were, covering the chase of the fabulous white beast from the earliest departure of the static hunters, their greyhounds, spears, and velvet jerkins, thin, incurved horns from which to blow success and terror through the forests of millefleurs, past the weaving of the beast at bay, goring a hound, paws raised in an ecstasy of indifference, all the way to the death of the unicorn, who stood finally docile in the courtly enclosure of its resurrection. The panoramic significance and passion of the symbolic chase, the dogs whose collars bore the monogram of Christ, the words *"Amour et Eternité"* pennanted in threads of gilt and silver for remembrance just above the men's plumed caps, were all belied by the profound and posturing dispassion of each animal and bird, the hunters even, who, for all the killing violence of their gestures, seemed equally detached from their stitched involvement, to look at nothing, only inward, as if meditating upon the great and open secret as it was there, in blinding detail, spread before them. The unicorn itself, shapely and dead white against the background of a thousand flowers, appeared no more than faintly amused throughout, appeared the one living thing to emerge unaffected at the end. The others, the hunters, in spite of their dispassion, looked worried with something if not with the hunt, sad for some reason if not their success, but the unicorn, even when unfurled, dead, over a horse's back, cast a gay, untroubled eye out from the rich space of wool and silk.

It was not as if Tristram had not viewed this countless times before, but wondering at each new figure that entered the hall, imagining him Steitler, looking at him questioningly, then back to the tapestries, he was struck, as he had not been earlier, by the anaesthetized rather than god-like detachment of the ceremonious pursuers and the mythical beast they pursued, whom he could not, for this reason, help but admire. It was barely clear even, he thought, who fled whom.

"Mr. Bone?"

He turned on the bench in the center of the room where he sat to discover beside him a dark young man who was so unlike whatever he had come to expect that he could not avoid a shade of incredulity in his voice.

"You are Paul Steitler?"

The person beside him was younger than he had imagined; "twice his age" Elizabeth had said when comparing him to her son, and he was obviously no more than five or six years the elder. Furthermore, to the degree to which his features seemed to lack the cunning, the mature, smiling unnaturalness which Elizabeth had led him to anticipate, he appeared better-looking. But, by his own statement, he was Paul Steitler. They walked together to a less conspicuous portion of the hall and sat down on a bench in the corner.

For Steitler too, the meeting was something of a surprise partaking largely of what he could not but imagine to be the grotesqueness that would necessarily, he thought, color whatever form Elizabeth's relationship with this extraordinary figure might take. From the note he had received, and the few remarks which Elizabeth had ventured on the subject, he had expected what he felt he had been promised, a fat man, but no one of such immensity as he had come upon sitting with his great head bared and his eyes half closed as if in prayer, dressed in light gray flannel, in the center of a long hall that seemed as dominated by him as by the richly hung walls. Nor had he been prepared for a setting of such magnificence. It seemed to him that wherever he looked there was either the great white unicorn in one stage or another of its death struggle amidst the swarming hunters or constantly, as though to complete his suffocation, Tristram Bone himself. In the face of all this he could not conceal a kind of helpless amusement in his tone as he spoke.

"You're certainly pulling out all the stops, Mr. Bone."

Tristram realized immediately that the interview would scarcely be facilitated by the fact that Steitler spoke a different language, and to augment his apprehension he noticed the faint smile that had accompanied his remark as the first evidence of something of the glib stealth he had come prepared to encounter. Nevertheless, he could not yet bring himself to dislike the young man or even to think of him in any particular way. If, Bone thought, he were indeed pulling out all the stops, and he was willing to admit this as part of his motive perhaps for having chosen the Cloisters for their meeting-place, Steitler had at least had the perception to remark it and, by speaking as he had, showed its effect as not entirely lost on him.

"I do what I can," answered Bone echoing the other's smile. He could not shake from him the sense of the brief, gallant encounter of single enemy soldiers in the midst of war, or the searching, tacitly sympathetic exchanges of strangers before they are introduced to one another, or when they are drawn into such curious and immediate intimacy by the occasion of some common misfortune like a rainstorm or the death of a friend. "I do what I can," he repeated, feeling that these were the friendly beginnings of whatever was to become their relationship.

"All I want to know," continued Steitler, indicating the tapestries with a gesture, "is whether I'm to take all this as real significant and symbolic. If the unicorn is here to help, I'd like to know about it."

"You do me an injustice," said Bone. "It's simply that we run no risk of being disturbed here. You may take the unicorn for whatever it may be worth to you."

"Well, I just wanted to know, is all," replied Steitler, "because I tend to bridle at this sort of thing. There seems to me a kind of arrogance in thinking life so easy that you've only got to stop short for a moment, keep your eye peeled, look sharp after years of indifference, and find right around you, in these tapestries for instance, the answer to most everything. I don't think things work that way; we're never going to have things so good, Mr. Bone."

"Just so." He had expected to explain to the young instructor why he had summoned him, but not why he had summoned him *here*. It was as if they had already returned to their respective colors, had left the awning for the clearing day, and it was suddenly a matter of knowing what to say next. The momentary, premature intimacy between them had been like a false spring, and it was again as if they had never met.

Steitler's problem was no less. Behind the meeting and the note which had of course referred to her, there was, he knew, Elizabeth. This was the fat man of whom she had spoken as having made love to her, the fat man who kept a monkey, and for some reason he had arranged this interview to speak of her. There were times when Steitler let himself think with much the same colloquial ease that marked his conversation, and he had passed the dull train-ride into the city by putting the whole matter to himself in the simplest terms possible. Out of his price range as he had decided Elizabeth to be, it was no less than proper that he pay to the extent to which he had become involved with her before realizing this. If seeing Bone, who, somehow, seemed to know of their involvement, was the payment required, he was willing to see it through. But already it was clear that here was more than he had bargained for.

The comparative ease of their meeting and, for the first

few minutes, of their conversation, was no true gauge to the shuddering effort with which Bone evidently addressed him now, reaching deep for his words, nor to the tensity and bewilderment Steitler found himself experiencing as he listened.

"Can you follow me," Bone was saying, once he had thanked the young man again for his kindness in coming, had expressed his disappointment that they might not have dinner together that evening, "can you follow me if I say that when people such as you and I meet there is no end to the amount of damage and hurt we can do to one another that will not, one day, be forgiven perhaps; that life is such that as long as we sin only against others like ourselves, who have finished growing up in it, we stand a chance at least of acquittal, but that with the young, the innocent, it is different?" Bone paused between what he had said and whatever he was about to say if there were no interruption, the interruption for which he seemed to plead with his hands poised motionless and anticipatory in the air, the fingers outstretched, his eyes wide and questioning. Steitler only nodded, the hands fell again to the knees, the heavy eyes turned from his face to the window at the far end of the hall. All that was clear to him was that the fat man loved Elizabeth as he himself did not, but that he should speak of her innocence, her youth—both of which in a sense existed, of course, he understood, gave her some of her son's invulnerability, were part of the charm by which she maintained the propriety, the

niceness of even the most unlikely situation—but that
he should speak of these qualities as though they rendered
her defenseless, the betrayed, was almost enough, for
Steitler, to make him cry out with a kind of dark amusement that there were things that Tristram apparently
did not know. Yet it was without amusement that the
young man nodded for Bone to continue uninterrupted
because he spoke with a kind of sincerity so passionate
as to make him feel guilty to seem any the less concerned
in response, himself.

"And I think," Bone proceeded, "that love, even when
it is true love, can be such a sin beyond forgiveness if we
direct it towards those who are not yet prepared to meet
its demands or, perhaps, towards those who are not prepared to overlook them in the manner of others who may
have been loved before. I can only say that somehow,
somehow, innocence must be protected for as long as it is
possible, and certainly neither you nor I, Mr. Steitler,
can dare to risk harming it—for the sake of our own souls
if not of those we harm." Bone's voice was vibrant and
deep, and he spoke slowly, though not, as in the case of
Steitler, whose slowness was even greater, as if he were
thinking ahead, controlling the intermittent silences, but
rather as if weighing and wondering at what he was saying
even as he said it, making use of the intermittent silences
to reflect upon his own words.

"I think," the young man answered, "that under some
circumstances people can harm other people, but those are

very rare circumstances sometimes involving people who are in love, as you say, but more often children, or criminals, and none of these—" Bone interrupted him not with any word but by raising his hand almost inadvertently with the effect of making the young instructor stop to consider what he had said. "You say I am something of all three?" Steitler asked, forgetting whatever he had been on the point of adding, with real wonder in his words. He found himself remembering vaguely how at some moment during the rather drunken conversation by the lake he had declared that lovers, like elephants, didn't forget, were bigger and better than most anybody else, could see farther and last longer, and here, beside him now, was the proof of his image, the greatest elephant of them all, a kind of passion behind each ponderous phrase, yet for all his previous perception Steitler felt pathetically unable to guess at what the huge, gray figure expected from him. He searched the bolted face.

"That is my question," said Bone.

"But look here, we're all grown-ups!" For the first time Steitler felt trapped by the situation, forced to pay more than he owed, and there was indignation in his voice. "Not children, not criminals. I don't know what Elizabeth has told you, or why she doesn't feel she can deal with me more directly, but after all, whatever you've made of it, it's only important up to a point. You go too far!"

"My concern, then, goes farther than yours."

"For Christ's sake," Steitler spoke the words not rapidly,

as an oath, but with the precision of an entreaty, "go somewhere else with your concern—there's a whole damned world full of really black sins for your trouble."

Bone sat silently, staring down before him, his hands hanging loose between his knees, leaning slightly forward as though at any moment he might tip over and go crashing through the floor, but there was no anger in his expression as he looked up at Steitler.

"I go where I am most needed—and where I need most to go." Steitler gave a short sigh of resignation and touched his damp forehead with a handkerchief. The day was humid and gray, and even in the comparative coolness of the monastery they were both aware of it.

"I hardly know you, Mr. Bone, but surely you take all this, and yourself, more seriously than anyone else is going to be willing to."

"Can you begrudge me that, when you say yourself that there will be no one else? Mayn't I, there being no other so reliable, so willing, stand as my own witness?" The young instructor, still full of his measured indignation, had allowed himself to speak as strongly as he had because it seemed to him that Bone's flesh became suddenly as armor about him, and that it would require the strongest word to pierce it; but as soon as the older man replied with the question that appeared so truly to look for an answer, he regretted his error, wished himself away from the transparent, blue-green eyes upon him. "Yet it's not of myself that I speak," Bone continued, "but of you, and

the danger, the harm of your affection." Steitler's sense of
being wronged passed, and he felt weak and young in the
overwhelming presence of the enormous figure.

"Can't you see that Elizabeth is no child," he pleaded,
"she is her own protection? There is no human change that
is not sad, but she, of all of us, doesn't change, and for
you, perhaps even for me, there is sadness, only no danger,
no harm."

"But I'm not speaking of Elizabeth!" For the first time
Bone's voice seemed to come alive, and with it Steitler's.

"Who then?" he caught out quickly for whatever he
might get.

"Her son." The words rang sharp in the young man's
ears. "It *is* the boy?"

In an instant of understanding he saw what it was Bone
asked—was he, Paul Steitler, in love, not with Elizabeth,
but with Lee, Leander Poor? He answered nothing at once,
and it was not because he was stunned by his realization.
It was rather that he was not stunned that confounded
him. Silence returned to the hall where they sat and slowly,
almost as in a dream, it was Lee's image that came uppermost to his mind. The boy might have been standing in
front of the tapestries, his hair bright against the darkness
of the forest where a tiny monkey, proud in his plumes,
ignored the kill, so clearly did Steitler see not only him
but, more suddenly, the possibility of being in love with
him as not entirely absurd. With only a few of the subtlest
yet most thundering changes somewhere deep within him

it could have been so, he could have answered Tristram
haltingly, with his misted smile, saying yes, yes, you are
somehow right; that was, though I never guessed it, my
secret; I am in love as you say. But though this was only a
twist from reality it was, nevertheless, unreal, not true.
With a felicity of emotion rare to him, a nearness to what
might to his own stupefaction have become tears involving
not only all that confronted him now but everything at
which he had never permitted himself to weep before,
Steitler understood that to be as accurate as the silent
figure beside him cried out that he be, he should say, oh
you are nearly right, my friend, you have come infinitely
close to finding out some particle of the truth, you are
only just wrong. But as a man charged with killing another
will not risk saying that he has perhaps, dimly, wordlessly,
contemplated murder, Steitler answered simply.

"You are wrong."

There was almost no more for either of them to say.
Bone apologized for what he called his particular illness
that had made him seek Steitler out before he had a right
to, and the young man offered one of his own for having
spoken in such bad taste, but they were not drawn nearer
by the exchange. To a degree they were both the wiser,
for Bone knew, and Steitler guessed, that Elizabeth had
lied and lied extravagantly in her own defense, but neither
could speak through the air heavy with doubt of what had
fallen even deeper within them than that realization.
Tristram could not ask what he wanted most to know,

whether Elizabeth and the young instructor were in love then themselves; and Steitler, who knew the answer and how desperately Bone listened for it, could not phrase it if only because he was fearful of making his own position seem any more precarious and strange than it already was; afraid of what Bone, of what Elizabeth, of what he himself might deduce from his saying no, he was not in love with her either. To this extent her device for silencing him had been successful: he did not, after all, betray her by saying that it was all perhaps a question of something less than love. Nor was he able, to himself, to say to what extent his friendship with Leander would be changed by what had been suspected of them, by his own brief, visionary insight, or to what extent he must be honest with the boy about all this, about his mother.

However, they arose, the curious pair, Steitler, spare and dark, with Tristram, speaking none of what passed through their minds, and walked through the monastery together, away from the tapestries with their indifferent hunters, the dispassionate unicorn, talking only of whatever might appear at the bottom of a flight of sagging stairs or around the corner of a dim arcade. They wandered through the chapel, where Bone managed to go no further than to reach out and touch the wooden robe of the one-handed saint who continued to stare slightly upward, his lips half parted, as they passed him, and Steitler stopped to admire the intricacy of the choir stall with his fingers and to remark, with something of his former ease, that great art was not, after all, for the tourist trade. Only when at last they reached the ramparts that looked out over the river far below and where they would leave one another for their separate cars did it become necessary for them to speak again as something more than people who had simply met and might depart never perhaps to meet again.

"And what of Lee?" Steitler asked as they stood there in the daylight, "what of him now?"

"What do you mean?"

"I mean what do we protect him from now, knowing what we know?"

Bone did not answer immediately but leaned his elbows on the thick stone bulwark, looked out into the stifling grayness, and did not turn as he spoke. "I'm not certain. Innocence must be somehow protected, that is all I can think."

"I think he should be told." Steitler joined him at the wall, following the direction of his eyes out across the river, the high cliffs on its far side.

"Everything?"

"Not perhaps everything, but what his mother gave you to believe, so he can know something of what it's like to be alive here, now."

"That would not be my way," and as Bone spoke he turned, which put his pale, heavy face so close to his listener's that Steitler seemed to see it all for the first time. There was so much of him, the young man thought, that one had to take it in gradually, like a landscape, guessing at distances and perspectives. He was a freak really, a show-off, yet how important that observation might be he could not tell any more than how important it was for his students to know that Dr. Johnson was scrofulous and had the sight of only one eye, Pope a hunchbacked dwarf, Milton blind, facts that were either of first significance or almost none.

"But my way is my own and I will force it on no one," Bone added. Steitler could not help wondering what indeed was his way, what were his slow aspirations—to be the great, white moon of her menopause perhaps, the huge and sweet chevalier of Elizabeth's middle-age—but at the irrepressible vulgarity of his conjectures he felt so much the same mixture of wild amusement and horror as he had experienced upon hearing Motley's explanation of show-offs that he resolved to leave quickly before they should get the better of him.

"Well, we can each of us do no more than what seems best, I imagine," said the young instructor. "Like the poet says, it's a strange life."

"You will think kindly of me then?" Bone fingered a white handkerchief that hung limply from his breast pocket, where Emma had put it, as he spoke. For an answer Steitler only smiled as they shook hands, put his hand for a moment on his companion's shoulder, and then left him.

"My dear Elizabeth," wrote Bone once he had returned to his apartment, "I have just come from seeing Paul Steitler, and my purpose here is simply to offer you my as-

surance that there is no need for the concern which you
expressed to me when last we met. He has said that he
will speak to Leander so that they may know together
the extent to which their friendship renders them suspect,
and that they may make whatever adjustments seem necessary in face of that. It is my hope that this will put you
at greater ease." He then copied the note over again
neatly, and tossed the original towards the waste-paper
basket which it missed. The monkey scampered over to it
and, mimicking his master's gesture, tossed it several
feet farther away.

It was Emma's evening off, and she consented to deliver
his message to Mrs. Poor's door on her way down town.
There were cold things in the ice-box for his supper, and
she trusted that he had enjoyed himself that afternoon,
in the country was it? He answered absently that he had,
not thinking to correct her in either particular, wondering
only if the rose on her hat could be real, deciding upon
closer scrutiny that it wasn't. Good-bye. Good-bye.

They sat silently together in the living-room as it grew
dusk, the monkey and his master, and Bone felt curiously
aloof, as if he were suddenly detached from all but the
inner, factless actuality of all that was happening, had
happened, was perhaps now over and done. Could it be,
he mused, that the reliable witness he had prayed for
when kneeling before the crippled saint, the mirror able to
retain what it reflected like the one with the dark, gilded
eagle spread above it before him now, were at fault insofar

as they recorded all the facts when it was, after all, possibly something at another level that more crucially mattered? Was he as foolish as was the bird-fancier and his notes to continue a ponderous quest for a kind of accuracy, a true recording of all that went on? But no, he was not. It was the facts that would absolve him if he were to be absolved, would show him innocent or sinning, hunter or hunted, and it was the trivial, trammeling, torturing facts, as of his reflected enormousness, that would allow him finally to sink down and away, free, or to rise, as he suddenly thought of it, above the rough surface, into air or airlessness. The lightless languor of his thoughts was interrupted only by the panic of the doorbell which he roused himself to answer to find before him a messenger with a telegram.

It was from Maroo. She would arrive in the city the next afternoon unknown to Elizabeth, about whom she was concerned, and would Tristram meet her at the station at a certain hour? It took some minutes for him to absorb this new intelligence, but, when he had, it was to the destruction of much of what had seemed the sudden liberty and peace of the lonely evening. Maroo was coming, somehow she must know something of whatever there was to know, more probably everything, and what he had thought over and done with was not so at all. Such an old, old lady, he came near to saying out loud to himself, to come so far, on a train called the Blue Mountain, out of the south, into the north.

The monkey, who had followed him from the door back to the writing table, crouched beside him engrossed with the carpet.

"Look at me, little ghost," said Tristram, but the monkey petulantly refused.

"Look at me, old comic, Simon, my one and only." The animal did not move so that Bone finally reached down from his chair, took the little head in his hand, and forced it up to face him. The neck felt warm and precarious in his grip which he relaxed slightly as Simon clutched at his gray sleeve like the memory of childhood.

"Maroo is coming, my lad," he said, "she is coming tomorrow, and what, tell me what, do we make of that?"

C H A P T E R

XV

WHEN Elizabeth had taken her lorgnette to be fixed she was persuaded to replace the tortoise-shell frame with one of old silver, and through this she brought herself finally, on Thursday afternoon, to read the note which Emma had left during her absence the night before. She lay on a chaise-longue in her bedroom covered with an antique yellow Spanish shawl and regretted peevishly every necessity, the note chief among them, that postponed the sleep she sought. Having read it once she tore it up and let the fragments fall from her hand, some to clutter the ash-tray at her side, others to lie undecipherable upon the carpet.

It had been somehow part of Elizabeth's education as a girl, having something to do with her manner of talking, which was equally charming and facile whatever it lacked in perception or brilliance, something more to do with long observation of Maroo's peculiarly serene grace, to be able as a rule to transcend the disagreeableness of any situation, and to be almost always able to manage to overlook, sometimes to the extent of being completely unaware of it, the possibly unattractive, unusual, or simply difficult and confusing depths of anything she found happening about her. Generally true as this was, however, there were occasions when, for all the vagueness of a smile committing her to neither approval nor disapproval, hurt nor indifference, she felt to a deeper point and merely concealed a painful awareness of whatever she might find there. As Steitler had surmised, she might well have been able to brush successfully past her memory of their night together, might have been able to overlook it as a kind of lovely accident, but a number of things conspired against her.

There was, for instance, an almost physical sense of recovering from a sickness, of recuperation made none the easier by her inability to speak of it as such, to garner the sympathy it needed. When she lay in her bed at night or, as now, upon her chaise-longue, awaiting what seemed an invalid's respite, her body would move temperamentally with a kind of petulance, and she would fold her pillows again and again like letters asking not for love but only for understanding. There should, she thought, be someone to understand and to console, yet, instead, there was no more than what amounted, for her, to a malicious conspiracy. She would feel one leg soft through silk upon another, the dark hair brittle against her neck, and come close to shedding the hot and stinging tears of indignation, of someone who is suddenly and without reason neglected and

hurt. Then there came the afternoon with Tristram at the
aviary and all she had found herself crying out in her defense, and then, to complete what seemed the injustice
being done her, the note telling that her enemies had now
met and would soon search out her son, the cruellest stroke
of all. It became a matter of no great difficulty to think in
terms of warfare and revenge.

What she had said of Leander and Steitler she imagined,
in retrospect to have been said in justifiable revenge. Steitler had had no right to do whatever he had done, and her
own uncertainty strengthened rather than diminished her
hate. Tristram himself had been unforgivable enough to
have hounded her with the matter when escape was impossible, and then to pursue it even farther still, to see the
arch betrayer and write her of it, saying that he hoped it
would put her at greater ease, knowing the falseness and
horror of his own words, was too much. If this was their
revenge, somehow she must take after them with weapons
of her own, she must pursue them across fields as windy and
ringing as those behind the atrocious bird-house, slay
them with the axe of her torment and wrath, avenge her
son whom they might as well have slain with their cunning
prattle and malice. Let them kneel and pray for mercy to
see her adamant, tyrannical only in her own defense.
Weak, helpless, hapless Tristram she could fell with no
more than a look or a word, and, as for Steitler, she had
only to continue hinting at what she could call her suspicions to ruin him most irrecoverably. Let them beware.

The passion of her thoughts was disturbing, tiring, even to herself, and during the days since she had last seen Bone she looked for refuge as much from them as from their cause, for solace wherever she could hope to find it. She slept a good deal, arose late, took naps in the afternoons, and tried to quiet there what would not be quieted. She had seen George Motley too, had dined with him only the evening before, as the one person left to whom she could still turn. Without ever speaking of it, he let it be apparent, guessing at what he had not yet learned, that he knew all there was to know of what troubled her, and without more than an occasional, wistful smile, a hand laid for an instant upon hers, made it clear that he, at least, was on her side; that to him, if to no one else, it made no difference. Committing herself no farther than he, she showed her gratitude by confiding in him many of her minor likes and dislikes, with promise, if he continued faithful, of more to come. The tacit sympathy of their relationship became the one emerging success to which she could point. Otherwise she felt frighteningly alone. Several evenings before, she had gone even so far as to telephone Maroo long distance simply to hear her voice and gain whatever reassurance from it she could, and though the old lady was surprised, had been able to say little to help because her daughter told her nothing, Elizabeth was again brought almost to tears at merely the sound of her words cracking across so many miles.

With help, with care lavished, if by no one else, by herself, with the destruction of Steitler and Bone, she might recover, and with this hope she had laid herself down beneath the yellow shawl with the note which would, she imagined before opening it, ask only forgiveness. But no, no, it made her forgiveness utterly impossible instead. Steitler was apparently going to speak to Lee, and how much, how much would he say? To what extent would he be guilty of murder? With the torn paper scattered beside her, she turned over on her side, buried her face in one of the small velvet cushions heaped about her, and tried again to sleep. She was hindered in this by the maid who appeared at her door to announce that Mr. Bone was waiting for her in the living-room.

Tristram, some hours before, had arrived at the railroad station somewhat in advance of the time when Maroo's train was due. He decided that it would be less disturbing to go early and face the moving crowds of travelers and luggage, watch the hundred arrivals and departures that would tend to keep him occupied in themselves, than to remain at home simply waiting and thinking until it should be the proper time to leave, and as he descended slowly on an escalator into the immense well of the station, the complex activity beneath him seemed to confirm the wisdom of his decision. It would be difficult, he imagined, in face of all that, to think of anything but what was going on in such extravagant detail before him. Once he stepped from the moving staircase onto the shiny floor of the tremendous, vaulted room modelled after some famous

Roman baths with its distant ceiling of glass from which
a kind of submarine light fell in slow nets, he felt the
comparative insignificance of his own enormousness and
for a few moments was indeed as lost as he had hoped to
be in merely observing some part of his intricate, shifting
surroundings.

In and about the queues and clots of people sidled Negro
women in slacks pushing brass, shovel-like brooms with
which they scooped up the unending amounts of refuse
silently, as it seemed, since the particular noise of the metal
being scraped across the polished marble was as much
absorbed as every other particular noise, every single
human voice, into the vast, general, wordless hubbub of
countless voices and shuffling feet, the cries of porters,
warning announcements of time and place droned from
loudspeakers high above, and even the dull, vibrant roar
of trains somewhere below all this. A group of small boys
who came sliding vociferously down the broad rail between
the two escalators forced him to move forward, and with
difficulty he started to thrust his way through little clumps
of luggage and their single, dazed guardians, through hectic, passionate, swift farewells and greetings, in the direction of the information booth, which stood somewhere
before him in the center of the great room. He reached it
finally, discovered that Maroo's train was on time and
that he had about a half an hour to wait, found an empty
spot on the base of a huge column and sat down there,
placing his hat on his knee, to pass the time anaesthetized

by all that went on about him. But his thoughtless involvement with that chaos did not last, for he saw that instead, overwhelmed with its variety and magnitude, he
was forced more deeply within himself than by the somehow lesser solitude of sitting alone in an empty room. He
recognized suddenly in every face that passed him the
reflection of what appeared a similar, lonely, speechless
concern not with the station and the mechanics of arriving, departing, meeting someone, or saying good-bye, but
with something more vital still and far beneath such minor
embassies. He seemed to see in each figure that hurried by
a kind of indifference to all but some secret, unexpressed
care having little to do with their involving context. How
easily they could all, he thought, and himself with them,
be transported by some miracle to an altogether different
realm or dimension without noticing it perhaps for years
to come, continuing for centuries ignorant of their metamorphosis as they persisted in looking only inward, severed
always from no matter what new element might come to
replace the one through which they now with such detachment moved. Only the children, of whom there were not
many, appeared aware and truly to belong to their surroundings, for the over-excited games they played, dashing
in and out among the legs of their elders, trying to run
up the escalator that moved only down, and the like, were
after all special games that could be played nowhere but
in the station by people who remembered that it was in
the station they were. As for the others, great numbers of

them moved past, slowly or rapidly, singly or in groups, carrying bags and parcels, asking for directions, perusing time-tables, searching for something familiar like the face of a friend or the name of a particular town cranked up in red and gold to the iron frames above the entrance to each track, but their eyes seemed glazed and half unseeing to Bone who watched them, as unsuccessful in their various searches as they were unconcerned with that failure.

He resolved to think, contrary to his plan, about Maroo, all that had probably obliged her to make the trip, and all that there would have to be said between them, as the lesser of two evils, the greater of which would be simply to continue his unsettling observation of the crowds before him and their curious dispassion, which became his as he watched it. But such a change of direction was more easily decided upon than effected, and he found himself struggling with both matters at once, the dispassion of the crowds that had become partially his already versus the urgency and demands of Maroo's imminent arrival, all that had probably occasioned it, and all that it would probably occasion. It became a question of overcoming the first in order to prepare himself for the second.

He tried to anticipate the easiest and least painful way of helping a very old lady and her luggage out of the swarming station into a taxi, and then home, wherever that might be. Would she plan to stay with Elizabeth, he tried to wonder, even though she had apparently not told her daughter that she was coming? Would she know all of what had gone on the past week or so, his own part in it, Elizabeth's, even Steitler's? But he could not answer his questions, it remained for whoever was nearest her great age to guess at her motives, and he could not even venture possible answers with any great clarity. There was so much else right about him that demanded his attention or inattention, whatever it should be called. It was nearly possible to see all those people as engaged in a huge and complicated dance, moving in slow figures from which a kind of pattern might almost be deduced. In a bare patch of the shining, marble desert, not far from where Bone sat, there was an elderly woman who reminded him somewhat of Emma sitting on a black suitcase with a paper bag in her lap, and when she arose, picked up the suitcase, and started off towards the far side of the room, it was not long before a young man with a tennis racket and raincoat took her place. Were there, Bone wondered, similar shifts all through the station because this Emma-like woman had moved on; but it was not, of course, as simple as that. One of the iron gates from which steps descended to the level of the trains themselves opened, and an entire herd of travelers poured out to head in different directions. Some wandered aimlessly through the crowds as if unaware of the weight they carried, others speeded up stairways or down corridors with what passed for a purpose, a few seemed never to move farther than the gate itself, lost somewhere in the confusion of the greetings with which they were received as they emerged, and all were variously

absorbed into the crowds, but there seemed to be no re-
sulting compression, the young man with the tennis racket
could continue his measured, circular tour of the undimin-
ished patch of bare floor.

For a moment, watching this, Bone had to strain to
keep from rising to his feet, stretching his arms to their
full length above his head, and shouting with all his
power so that his voice might fill the whole enormous room,
his words resound from the vaulted, glass ceiling and the
massive columns, telling them to stop, stop, see where and
who they were, where and why they were going; to awake,
take notice, awake, awake, and discover that they were
men and women in a station, passionately involved with
trains, with arrivals and departures, and no more. But,
instead, he managed to think again of the old woman he
had come to meet, looked from one broad staircase to
another that he might find the easiest to climb with her,
glanced at his watch, and saw with a start that it was time,
her train was due, he must move on.

He wheedled permission from a uniformed guard to
descend to the track ahead of time, and was standing on
the platform with only a few others, porters, a man in a
wheel-chair and several children, as the head-light of the
train appeared far down the dark tunnel approaching
them. It rolled forward with infinite slowness and pains,
but there was still the uncontrolled clanging of steel against
steel, the uneven excitement of a hidden bell, and a vibra-
tion that shook the heavy platform and all who stood upon

it, waiting, as the locomotive passed and then stopped
with a kind of final, conclusive noise of cars butting softly
against one another, and countless energies falling back
into place. In an instant the nearly empty platform was
teeming with passengers, two-wheeled carts filled with
luggage, conductors crying out the name of the city as
though there were someone to hear it, and Bone peered
as best he could over the innumerable heads to catch sight
of Maroo as he walked towards the rear car.

His feeling of wild excitement, almost of dread, seemed
frighteningly more to him than the occasion justified as
from almost a stupor he came suddenly to the sense of
keenest, most defenseless animation. Though he had seen
her less than a month before in the South, he wondered if
he would recognize Maroo, if she would recognize him, if
perhaps her telegram were not all a hoax or a hallucination,
and his being here now the emblem of his final disintegra-
tion, something from which he must awake, but there!—
right beside him!—yet so old, so old and ancient a figure,
it could not be, but was; she was there, beside him, now.

"Maroo!"

"Oh, bless you, dear lad, for coming! Now where is that
black citizen with my things . . . ?" She turned, as if
forgetting him completely for an instant, or not yet fully
aware that they had met, just as he was about to embrace
her, but then back, quickly, to become almost lost in the
folds of his coat as he pressed her for a moment to him, as
she patted his immense back with her slim, old hand. For

the first time in as long as he could remember tears filled
Tristram's pale eyes as spontaneously as though he had
been struck cruelly across the face. "How are you, dear
boy! You've no idea how good it was to find you right
here, and on time . . ." There was no reason for the tears
that had never left his eyes, but he was nonetheless un-
done by them even though Maroo had not noticed while
her voice came haltingly and frail, her head trembling un-
controllably as she spoke, wondering about her things,
tipping the porter, and looking so helplessly, bravely, at
the people crushing their path up the stairs that Bone
wanted to take her up in his arms and cudgel with his
free fist a way of escape for them. "I have so much to tell
you, Tristram, but oh let's wait till we can get away from
all this!"

For fear that his voice might betray more of his feelings,
which would only embarrass the old lady so involved still
with her voyage and getting away to where it would be
quiet again, so without such sudden, sick floods of sentiment herself, he simply repeated again how good, good it
was to see her, asking her again how she was, begging her,
without speaking it, to reassure him, that she would, for
all her great age, the terrifying helplessness about her, sur-
vive this turmoil, the crowd, the clumsiness of his inarticulate reception.

The station, which was despair enough seen through
what had been his detachment, the queer recognition of a
similar detachment in all the others who wandered about

there, became something even more menacing as he guided
Maroo through it, her large suitcase in his hand, the perspiration wet on his forehead. She had caught a cold on the
train, she said, the air-conditioning had gone off and then
on all night, and her cough, harsh and painful, only added
to his apprehensions that they would never reach the street.
He kept looking about to make certain that she was still
following him as he cleared a way towards the main staircase, and though her smile was reassuring, her eyes placid
and untroubled, he saw her as so old, so much older than
he had remembered her, that surely the effort required of
her would be too great, he would have to find some other
way. But his fears came to nothing, for, helping her up
the wide, marble stairs, stopping every few steps so that
she could catch her breath, he finally reached the open day
with her and without too much difficulty found a taxi in
which, at last, she could breathe more evenly again and
her voice became steadier. She had said that her plan was
to go directly to Elizabeth's even though she was not expected there, and Bone gave the address to the driver
telling him to take the road through the park as quieter and
greener than any other.

"You see, Elizabeth telephoned me," she said, her arm
extended through the loop on the car wall at her side, her
hand, mottled and thin, hanging loose as she rubbed the
tips of her thumb and forefinger gently together, "earlier
this week, and it was evident that she was very distressed
about something though she did not say what or even

that she was distressed at all, nor did I press her. Yet, of course, I knew." Bone half expected her to turn towards him at this to show that she knew him somehow involved too, but she did not. Her lids were very heavy, but her eyes, her mournful French eyes as she called them, were bright and awake as she looked out at the grass, the benches of people with their faces turned towards the sun and the children playing about them. "So I decided to come north, which I've had in my mind to do for some time anyway, and put myself at rest about her." It was mercifully unnecessary for Bone to add anything to this; she required for the moment no answer from him, but talked on, very much as she wrote, about how she had left— they had all thought the dear old soul a little out of her wits to go to the city just as it was about to become unbearably hot, she said—and how she had had to laugh at the waiter on the train who insisted upon calling her Miss. But in spite of the grace and charm of what she was saying, Bone could not help but listen only partially much as he felt she was speaking herself only half hearing her own words, and thinking instead of all she wanted eventually to say about something else.

As he watched the old lady who had once been as tall as Elizabeth but slumped now, her head still trembling not quite imperceptibly as she spoke on, he thought he understood why he had almost wept upon meeting her. Seeing Maroo, whose brown face bore what seemed a century of wrinkles sewn by every possible reaction to every possible situation, whose black, three-cornered hat fastened with a jet pin could not dim the glitter of profound consciousness in her hazel eyes, he realized that he had shed tears because, to him, the greatest wrong of all was that she had felt compelled to come north and implicate herself in one more situation whose greatest sin was to be unworthy of her concern. If such diseased and perhaps trivial intrigue, for intrigue it was, could come to involve even such a presence as this, then what hope was there for any of the others? What hope might there be for himself, Tristram wondered, for Elizabeth and her lover, if this ancient, precarious relic could be caught up into their doings, and drawn by their machinations into this position of subservience? There could be little, or there could be none. Hopelessness, in spite of all that had happened, was new to him. It made seeing Elizabeth again easier yet more difficult. Would she recognize the implications of her mother's presence?

For Tristram, Maroo's presence implied an end of sorts, merciful, yet in its finality somehow hopeless. It was as if, for him, the arrival of the old lady unbelievably encumbered with age, a cold in her trembling head, her chest, marked the last point the situation could reach at the level on which it had so far taken place. In order for it to reach farther, for the intrigue to persist beyond this ultimate, conclusive present which had managed as a final trick to involve the uninvolvable, Maroo, it would require another level altogether, would need in some manner to seek out an entirely new plane or dimension for its involutions. He felt, as the taxi drew up to the curb before their destination, that this was a last gesture of despair.

"I'm not going to let you off scot free, Tristram," said Maroo as they approached Elizabeth's door, "now that you have seen me to my new diggings where, once before, scouting around and amongst alien furniture, I managed so painfully to stub two toes on an accursed chair that my foot swelled up beyond the confines of my oldest and loosest shoe. I'm grateful to your strong right arm for getting me here, up all those stairs with all my worldly belongings, and you were a good lad to do it, but I'm not going to let you off yet. Whatever the trouble is, there are things I shall need you to tell me that Elizabeth never will, so may I invite myself to dinner as old ladies can, just the two of us, and the monkey of course, as soon as possible, tomorrow evening perhaps?" She looked up at him uncertainly for his answer while he rang the doorbell, as though she would go no farther until he spoke.

"It will be my great and undeserved pleasure. You don't know what it means to have you here, Maroo."

"Splendid then. I shall don my gladdest rags, such as they are, and arrive at your building around seven."

The door opened, and they were ushered in by Elizabeth's maid. Tristram walked on into the living-room while Maroo stayed in the dim hall to unpin her hat before a mirror. The maid, to whom the old lady's indentity was unknown, announced simply the presence of Mr. Bone to her mistress, who lay covered with a yellow shawl in her bedroom, trying to sleep. In a moment she arose, slipped on a violet dressing-gown, and came out to meet him. Bone stood in a patch of sunlight on the gray carpet, his hands behind him, his face in shadow.

"Really, Tristram, I've no idea why you're here. It seems to me you've done us all enough damage as it is." Her voice was hard and her face as immobile as his. He made no answer.

She had seen, of course, when she spoke, only Tristram. But then as though not sufficiently punished by his slow, melancholy presence for the ugliness of her words, she saw, and managed somehow to recognize, who else was witness to her humiliation, Maroo advancing from the groin of the hall as she had never, for Elizabeth, advanced before.

With a quick, impoverished cry the younger woman ran to her mother and fell weeping on her neck. "There, there," said Maroo, "there, there, my dear. There, there," and over Elizabeth's throbbing shoulder nodded to Bone, who, without a word to either of them, started slowly to leave the room. Tomorrow at seven, her glance said, the lines about her mouth making almost a smile or, rather, a question of her unspoken words. Tomorrow, tomorrow, dear lad?

He replied with a barely visible inclination of his bared head as the hall received him. The last thing he heard as he closed the door gently behind him was the wordless murmur of Elizabeth's sobbing, and Maroo's helpless cough.

CHAPTER
XVI

Maroo was late. By eight o'clock the next evening she had not yet arrived, and candles burned expectantly from the table that had been set in the living-room for their dinner with a lace cloth and the best china, silver and glass that Emma could find. The curtains were drawn, and the only other light came from two more candles which had been placed for the occasion in the tall, silver holders on either side of the fireplace. The silence was complex with reflections of the motionless flames and anticipation.

Both the monkey and his master wore evening clothes. With the black of his dinner-jacket almost invisible against the dark background of the couch in which he sat, his head tilted back in shadow and the patent-leather of his pumps gleaming on the carpet before him, Bone's figure seemed fantastically broken and reassembled by darkness. The bright expanse of shirt-front became an enormous, starched mask with the corners of a bow-tie peering from beneath the folds of his chin as eyes, the two jet studs as nose and

230

tiny, frightened mouth, and then nothing distinguishable until the feet which appeared nightmarishly slender and incapable of propelling so vast a head. A gold seal hanging from his vest flickered with his heavy breathing in the candle-light. When his hands moved it was as if to claw off the mask.

The monkey crouched grave and motionless on the tiny, purple chair which had been drawn up along with two larger ones to the table. His lipless mouth was closed and his big eyes damply luminous under the silk hat fastened beneath his whiskers with a little bow. If he looked at any-thing, which was not certain, it was at his master.

When a bell finally rang it was not the door but the telephone, and the result of its ringing was to set a compli-cated mechanism in action. A second, pursed face floated up above the enormous mask, and the inadequate feet squirmed darkly as Bone arose. The monkey leaped from his chair and ran like a dwarf in panic at his own foppery towards the door. Emma, incensed at the thought of a good dinner near to ruin, stepped into the unlighted dining-room to listen. It was Elizabeth.

"I'm afraid mother can't possibly come. Her cold is much worse and she's running a high fever. The doctor has just left. There may even be danger of pneumonia." Her voice was flat and without emotion. "So you see it will be impossible for her to go anywhere for some time. She asked me to telephone you."

"I'm extremely sorry, Elizabeth, extremely sorry."

Bone's voice sounded unnaturally loud and dire to him in the quiet room. "I shall come by tomorrow to inquire after her if I may . . ."

"You must do as you like, Tristram. Lee is coming too, so you can see what a frightful, tragic position I am in, thanks to you." There was a pause, and he thought for a moment that she had gone.

"Elizabeth." There was no answer, but he felt certain now that she was still listening.

"Elizabeth!" He waited for her reply with the mouthpiece pressed so firmly to him that his lips were twisted into a kind of grimace as he called out her name again. He drew a sharp line in the blotter before him with his fingernail. Then he heard the click of the receiver as she slowly hung up.

"Emma, Emma!" he called so loudly that the monkey scampered from the threshold into the hall. In an instant she appeared, her apron starched and spotless, her hair drawn with care into an especially tight bun, her eyes wide.

"Emma, Mrs. Poor's mother is ill and will be unable to dine with us. Will you," he said, rising, "do us the honor of taking her place this evening?"

"Eat with you?" the line between her eyes deepened.

"Please."

"Oh, but that would not do, would not do." Bone well knew what passed through her mind. His long-standing invitation simply to sit in the living-room mornings when the sun poured in and he was either away or not yet awake

had so visibly shocked her sense of propriety that never
once, to his knowledge, had she accepted it, and he consequently understood that to allow herself now to dine with
him there would be clearly, for her, an even more flagrant
desecration of the sanctity of the master's premises or
Herrenstube as she called it. However, the struggle that she
was evidently sustaining as a result of the equal strength
of her curiosity encouraged him to press the point.

"Nonsense. If you will take off your apron and be kind
enough to put all the food on the table at once, you, Simon,
and I will simply have our dinner together. Do not dis-
appoint me, Emma."

"But I am in kitchen clothes, Mr. Bone. I cannot . . ."
her accent became especially thick at moments of crisis.

"That can be remedied. Please do as I ask." She turned
abruptly and left for the kitchen in a state of high agitation
which it was difficult to define as either indignation or delight. In spite of the length of their acquaintance, Bone
was not certain that she would return at all, but in the
event that she might he drew from a chest nearby the
twin to the Spanish shawl he had given Elizabeth some
years before on returning from Europe. This one was not
yellow but black, richly embroidered in silver thread with
flowers and birds, and he draped it over the chair that was
to have been for Maroo. The monkey had returned to the
scene, and he lifted him up and placed him, with warnings
to behave, on the far end of the table before sitting down
himself. To his surprise Emma reappeared shortly without

her apron, carrying a heavy tray, and Bone arose again to
help her into her chair and arrange the shawl over her thin
shoulders. Her expression was one of rapt bewilderment
as her employer poured the wine and their dinner began.

"Honor the ladies, my lad," he had said, and the monkey
tipped his silk hat to Emma.

In black and tinsel, sable and silver, she sat, straight as
any stick, as reticent as the most recently canonized of a
company of saints, observing that the new lightheartedness of her master, whose sleepy smile which she could not
yet properly return, was either her martyrdom or its
holiest reward. With much the same ease and sense of
success he had experienced when speaking of love to the
manicurist the week before, he addressed Emma in paragraphs now on what amounted to his sudden feeling of
miraculous reprieve, the bountiful conclusion to all that
seemed for so long to have troubled him. Maroo had not
come, nor would she for some time it seemed, nor would
she ever perhaps, and however profound his affection and
consequent concern for her welfare might be they became
irrecoverably fused with his love for the end of despair
which her absence this evening led him at last to consider
as possible. The situation in which she, her daughter and
the two young men were involved with him could con-
ceivably grow worse, but, for himself, Bone felt that he
could no longer grow worse, as it were, with it. Somewhere,
at some moment, possibly when he met the old lady's
train, he had reached the farthest limit of his susceptibility,

but this proved also to be the point from which painful descent was no longer possible; he could only rise now with a kind of gaiety, the lightheartedness perceived by Emma, as though he were on his way to being almost free again and, to the extent that he rose, disentangled from all the most recent intrusions of actuality. Yet this ascent into upper regions, this new sense, born largely from Maroo's failure to arrive, of escape from the encumbrances of his dilemma, was not anaesthetized and moribund as he had felt the dispassion of the crowds in the station and the hunters of the unicorn to be; instead, unlike them, he was passionately aware of the context that he fled, and that awareness gave brilliance and expedience to his flight.

As they sat over their dinner in the candlelight that glistened softly from his satin lapels and made a gentle mist of their faces, made gentle faces reflected in the misted brightness of silver and glass, Bone's words to Emma and the monkey were a translation of the sweet and difficult tongue of his thoughts. He spoke of the summer so soon to begin as the nearest approximation to the benison of his release, and told how they might all go to the coast of some northern state for the months when the city became unendurable with heat. They might take a particular house by the sea where, as a child, he had been and had floated, drawn on by the current, down small tidal rivers through deserts of white sand, his ears submerged, hearing only the water, his gaze on the sky which seemed bluer than any at least to an upturned, wet and wishing face. Gulls, herons, egrets, and roseate terns wheeled, screamed there above him, gray rocks and marsh grass of lightest green in the distance, he explained, nakedness, justified at last, blurred, bleared by the ocean that bore it. Summer was what they all needed, he said, and he spoke as though there were nothing dearer or more real to him than their need.

Throughout the meal he seemed to address himself more to the monkey than to Emma, and she noticed this, of course, with anger directed not towards Bone but towards Simon. It was the animal again who had the advantage, she thought. He was properly dressed, and she was not. The splendid shawl did not entirely conceal the shabby dress beneath it even when she drew it more tightly about her. He did not speak, and neither, for the most part, did she. His silence, however, befitted his species and if, as she had more than once suspected (and as had her employer too, she imagined), his powers of communication were considerably greater than he chose to have known, then his saying nothing would be taken as only one more indication of his superior wisdom. Her silence, on the other hand, would be interpreted correctly as no more than a sign of her inadequacy. But there was nothing she could do about all this. She must simply listen, with him, to whatever it was *der Knochen* was saying about summer, the ocean, and birds in the sky. She could not, as she so wildly wished, strike him down from his seat on the table.

The maniac smile with which he listened to his master, his eyes always glancing towards her, told her this.

The monkey's shy smile, his averted eyes, so charmed Bone that he was himself aware that it was to him rather than Emma he spoke. In the end they were, the two of them, his most reliable witnesses, he thought, but of the pair it was Simon that he most trusted and loved. He took the carnation from his buttonhole and tossed it into the middle of the table. The monkey took a violet from his and tossed it too. He was extraordinary was he not, Bone exclaimed. *Ja*, Mr. Bone.

The violet had fallen into a pitcher, and the monkey reached in with his skinny arm to retrieve it. When finally he managed to find it his fur was so covered with cream that as he tried to lick it off it whitened his whiskers and left his face pale as a clown's. Bone laughed delightedly, and wiped off what he could with his handkerchief. Simon tipped his hat once more to Emma. Bone followed the suggestion and, taking his eyes from the monkey with effort, turned to her himself to renew a conversation about many things, the heat of the city, the ocean of which she confessed her fear, the superiority of one's own house to any hotel however luxurious, yet they both spoke with a falsity born of the mutually recognized fact that though neither of them mentioned him, Simon was, in different ways, uppermost in both of their minds.

When they had finished their dinner, and Emma, her

shawl trailing the floor, brought in coffee and set it down before them, Bone drew back the curtains and opened wide the window nearest where they sat. He hoped by this device to set things right again. His first enthusiasm at what had seemed a new sense of freedom no longer prevented him from realizing that the evening was not progressing as pleasantly as he had anticipated earlier. Emma's discomfort and irritation were evident in countless ways as he watched her stiffly sipping coffee; the monkey's woebegone, neglected silence was made the more poignant by the finery he wore; the still air of the room itself appeared suddenly breathless and excessively warm, and to open the window occurred to him as a way of remedying all this. An unusually strong breeze billowed the curtains and whipped the candle flames down into bright slugs of fire. From the street below came the whistle of a doorman trying to hail a passing taxi and then two blasts of a horn. They sat in near darkness, the three of them, relieved by their observation of the night from having to make further conversation.

Bone drew the monkey to him and gently worried the fur on the back of his neck; Emma sat motionless with her hands folded on the table before her. The light from a window across the street cast a bright patch on the lace cloth, but their faces remained in shadow. The wind extinguished the candles.

It was in both of their minds that if the monkey were ever going to speak it would and should be now. Like fear or love it was in the pits of their stomachs and the excited acceleration of their hearts that if he spoke it would be intolerably of the past; not the jungle of his own chattering birth and capture, but the original realm of Bone's tiny purple and rosebud chair, the German grandmother who had looked more like a monkey than Emma remembered or chose to remember. In silence they awaited his first pronouncement. Bone drew back his hand.

Off the table leapt the monkey, the tails of his jacket flying out behind him and his silk hat knocked askew as he landed and leapt again to a streak of light that sprawled in widening, criss-crossed perspective on the floor in the center of the room so that Emma and Bone had to turn about in their chairs to see him spin around and around there making no sound. Only when, after a few minutes, he ceased spinning and simply crouched in the pale light, bouncing softly up and down, his fingers digging into the carpet, his tail curled out stiff, did he start to speak to them. He no more than muttered at first. Drawing his mouth into a small, flexible point way in front of his teeth, he made clicking, kissing noises so rapidly that no syllable was distinguishable from another. Emma called out his name loudly, and at the sound of another voice he threw his head back and screeched in short bursts more like a bird's than an animal's, and of such shrillness that she clapped her hands to her ears with an exclamation and gave an agonized look at Bone, who sat unmoving in the darkness.

The monkey's screaming continued, his bouncing motion becoming wilder and more erratic. The table cloth fluttered towards him like hands in the wind. In another instant Emma jumped up from her seat, ran over to the little animal, and struck him with a heavy swing of her hand. He gave a last, surprised scream and leaped for protection to the lap of his master, who had been on the point of rising. The shawl slid from Emma's shoulders and fell, black and silver, to the carpet.

"What have you done!" Bone cried out to her, switching on a large lamp that flooded the room with light and revealed Simon quivering in the crotch of his arm. "He meant no harm! What have you done?"

She had not moved from the scene of her wrath, and remained there to answer him.

"It was too much, that's all. Too much."

Bone's first impulse had been to strike her to the floor, but he hesitated now, trying to understand what had happened. They seemed both so defenseless, the woman and the monkey, that he suddenly saw no other but himself as the offender. The guilt became illogically his own, and he stood there by the lamp, his thick shoulders sagging, unable to decide upon the proper word or action. Massive and white, thrust slightly forward over the starched shirt-front which had been dominant by candlelight, his face bore a helpless expression of something less than anger, more than apology. He neither smiled nor frowned, yet his mouth curved unnaturally.

"Well, let there be an end to it."

"So," answered Emma. She would not look at him directly but at the wall behind him. She moved now to pick up the shawl and start clearing the table.

"It was a very good dinner, Emma. Thank you for having it with me." He could not decipher her reply, but there seemed to be no resentment in her tone, at least none towards him. The atmosphere was easier again, and, saying good-night, he walked down the hall towards his rooms, still holding Simon cradled in one arm.

That the scene had not disturbed him more than it did continued to surprise Bone until he looked back on it a few moments later from his dressing-room. Simon had made loud, terrifying noises, and Emma had struck him. That was all. If, recognizing her irritation as he did, she had not struck him, or if he had made no noise and she had struck him anyway, it would have been another matter. But, as it was, the cause and the effect were both clear and articulate and consequently left no disagreeableness behind. Even his own momentary feeling that he had been himself the offender was clear too, at least to him, and made part of a pattern that he recognized. None of this was more than momentarily disturbing and, furthermore, it was over now. The monkey was not hurt, Emma would have recovered by morning, and he was again able to think of the evening as a pleasant one, the first in a new series. Much of his former lightheartedness returned.

He would go to Elizabeth's the next day as he had suggested to her over the telephone earlier, inquire after Maroo, possibly even see her, possibly see Leander too, certainly Elizabeth, and though this would be a dangerous test of what seemed to him the enlightened serenity of his position, he felt confident that he would lose nothing by it. His sense that all the participants in the events of the past week were alone within themselves to the extent that each was in some way separated by misunderstanding or reticence from all the others, became, for the first time, not a cause for despair but rather a kind of additional security. He was certain that among Elizabeth, Steitler, Leander, and Maroo there were no alliances, nor was he himself now particularly bound to any of them. It was as if a disease had been successfully isolated into a number of distinct areas so that none of them could be further plagued and the germs would die in isolation. There might be sadness but, more importantly, a kind of safety in the loneliness he recognized.

The animal crouched in a corner of the leather dressing-room couch where Bone had placed him and watched his master change from his evening clothes into his red dressing-gown. When this operation was finished Bone detached the watch chain and gold seal from his vest and went to place it in the top drawer of his bureau which, by some mischance, Emma had neglected in her cleaning. The disarray of objects there bothered him and, pleased with a dismay so easily dispelled, he set about to put it in order.

He tumbled some cuff-links into their little leather box,

drew out a ring of keys to take later to his desk, piled three monogrammed handkerchiefs in a corner, and replaced several business cards in an unused wallet. It was when he tried to push several pairs of gloves out of sight to the back of the drawer that he felt some hard object wedged in there. It turned out to be a flat, leather case which was familiar to him as a nearly forgotten possession but whose contents he could not remember. Forgetting his unfinished task he sat down on the couch beside Simon to puzzle over it. He refused to open it right away but turned it over and over in his hands trying to recall what it contained. A mystery so easily solved simply by the opening of a lid encouraged his prolonged speculation. Simon became as fascinated as he and reached out to touch the leather. Then Bone remembered, opened the case, and found that he was correct.

It was lined with blue plush and held a bone-handled straight razor bright with sharpness for all its disuse. For years he had neither seen nor thought of it, yet as soon as it was in his hand his fingers responded reminiscently to its minutest detail; the curve of the handle, the tiny bolt that held the blade in place, the groove into which it could be collapsed with a flicking motion of the wrist. He closed it and then opened it again. Turning it this way and that he made the light of the one lamp glisten on the keen steel.

Such an instrument, he thought, was encumbered with no more than two functions. You shaved with it, or you used it to cut your throat; in one way or another it was contrived to simplify life. To which of these ends he might have put it had he discovered it a few days before, the morning after Motley's visit for instance, was a subject with which he was able to amuse himself for some minutes, slumping comfortably in the couch with his bare feet stretched out before him, continuing to twist the razor slowly in the light. In the end, he concluded, he would not, probably, have become a suicide if only because long familiarity with the idea tended to make impossible the suddenness and novelty of conception that he imagined necessary to its enactment.

This realization comforted him. Perversely then he tried to dissuade himself. Might not long familiarity with the idea of suicide work equally well towards making transition to the act itself fatally effortless, almost imperceptible? But he had not discovered the razor several days before, he had discovered it now. Was such a death possible at this moment, he wondered.

With Maroo on the preceding afternoon it had occurred to him that there was no longer hope. If she could become implicated in this affair, then escape or survival was surely impossible for the rest of them, and it was, after all, only her failure to appear that evening that had restored his faith, had enabled him to envision an end apart from hopelessness. Yet, as he considered it now, her failure to appear because of illness only indicated her deeper involvement. Was not the fact that the old lady was ill, perhaps irrecoverably so, as a result of the voyage she had felt necessary to make, cause for a supreme despair, he wondered, Simon beside him, the razor in his hand. Bone put this to himself as strongly as he was able, but to no avail. In spite of all, he could not lose the giddy sense of having been somehow freed.

He tested himself with these thoughts but was not cast down by them from his new position, not of indifference, not of anaesthetized detachment, but of having risen in some manner far enough above the situation to see it clearly still, yet to be no longer in any way pained by it. He would test this position again on the next day by going to Elizabeth's. As a man who has suddenly recovered the use of a crippled limb cannot avoid trying its strength again and again, Bone reconfirmed this decision.

There was the top drawer of the bureau to finish arranging and to close, there were the lamp to be extinguished and the darkness of bed to be sought, but the razor in his hand delayed him. To some degree, in spite of his ultimate refusal of the solution it offered, it too must be used as part of a final test. His accidental rediscovery of it and its own exquisite sharpness forbade him merely to replace it, unproven, in its flat case. This was confirmed for him by the birds who stared down from their white frames about him and by the expectant immobility of Simon at his side. Almost against his will he held it at arm's length and then carefully drew its dull side across his throat. With the smooth, rounded edge of the blade he made the gesture of suicide. The safe back of the razor enabled him to simulate danger out of existence, and from ear to ear he slid it harmlessly.

The monkey, who had watched the scene intently, reached out, took it from him, and scrambled to the far end of the couch where he squatted with a band of high-light seaming his silk hat. Mimicking his master, he drew the blade across his own thin throat and then back again with a single, fierce gesture before letting it fall from his hand. It dropped to the slippery cushion, revolved once, and then slid to the floor.

His black palms fluttered like a child's as he listed back against the leather arm. His legs buckled loosely, and, opening his mouth wide enough to show his strong teeth, he gave a harsh, gargling cry.

It had not been immediately apparent, but in a moment, above his miniature collar, the swelling red line that followed in the razor's wake became visible. Monkey blood started to pulse down his shirt front. He arched his body back stiffly and tumbled from the couch. His hat rolled off and lay beside him on the floor where he twitched hideously so that the blood flowed with greater force onto the heavy carpet that absorbed it.

As if it were only at this point that Bone became aware of what had happened, the monkey's imperfect imitation of his own action, he struggled to his feet, flung open the door and bellowed Emma's name down the corridor before rushing over to where the little animal lay. He fell heavily to his knees beside him, pressed his hand to the ludicrously trousered legs in an attempt to quiet them and, when all movement seemed to have ceased except for the mouth which opened and closed in silence, picked up the small silk hat and half crawled, half fell with it into the darkness of his bedroom. The door swung closed behind him leaving the room to an unlikely silence that was broken only by the panicked clattering of Emma's slippers as she came running down the hall.

Standing on the threshold, her hair unpinned and falling down the back of her flimsy bathrobe, she thought the room empty at first until she caught sight of the monkey sprawled out in shadow. When she ran over and snatched him up in her arms his head fell back so grotesquely that in horror, and to her own horror, she dropped him, her ears ringing with the frail clicking of his throat as he fell on his back. Her face flushed and shining with tears, stains of blood at her breast where she had held him, she sank with a wild sob to the floor and tried to wipe his face clean with the hem of her robe. His breathing was imperceptible now, and all movement had ceased. Nothing she could do seemed of any use. The monkey was dying, or he was dead.

She smothered her face in her hands, and tears slipped down her fingers. Her shoulders shook with a grief that had actually no more to do with the fact of death as it lay before her in the form of the small, unraveled body, than with the pain of mourning a life so recently despised and, less recently, with the disfigured statue in the park that she had never found, and even the grandmother whose resemblance to the little animal, though never precisely identified by Emma as such, arose in her now with an inarticulate pang of sufficient poignance to add more hurt and greater dimensions than she knew to her sorrow as she knelt there on the floor by Simon.

Only after some minutes did she look up to see the razor where it had fallen near them and to wonder at the cause of the catastrophe, at the whereabouts of her employer and the nature of his crime or complicity. Still sobbing, but more absently now, she arose to her feet and knocked at the door to his bedroom. There was no answer. She knocked again with greater force.

"Mr. Bone!" she cried out, "Mr. Bone, something *awful* has happened!" She spoke the guttural, shaken language of terror. Again there came no reply, and, without looking back at the little figure lying in shadow upon the carpet, she pushed the door open and advanced timidly into the darkness.

CHAPTER

XVII

ALTHOUGH Steitler had said to Bone when they took leave of one another at the Cloisters that he thought Leander Poor should be to some extent enlightened about his mother and the situation which she had more or less created, he never went even so far as to tell the boy that the meeting had taken place at all. In spite of his earlier plan, he told him nothing, and this was largely because the alternative, to tell him everything, had come to seem impossible to the young instructor.

There was enough of a kind of excessive agitation and vulgarity, he thought, in the lengths to which the comparatively simple fact of his night with Elizabeth had already been brought as a result of her panicked denial and defense, the tortuous investigations of Tristram Bone, and his own unsuccessful meeting with that extraordinary figure, without his going even further, seeking out Lee, and explaining the entire matter into an even greater unpleasantness. Consequently, though he continued to see his young friend as frequently as before, he always avoided now mention of anything that might tend to make it necessary for him either to tell all that he knew or willfully to conceal it. Whatever successful communication had existed previously between the two young men was destroyed, if only in Steitler's mind, by the deception from which their friendship was forced now to proceed. He could no longer see Leander, and they saw each other often, without realizing that their relationship was being transformed into something new, something more like a game.

To strengthen this realization was his memory of the curious, near-revelation he had experienced when it became clear to him among the unicorn tapestries what it was that Bone had been trying to say about that relationship. The enormous gentleman had asked him if it could be that he loved the boy, and for a moment, to his own stupefaction, he had been unable to reply. For an immortal instant he had regarded what might otherwise have seemed an ugly accusation with a candor so profound that he was permitted the rare sight of a staggering and unsuspected truth about himself that he came extraordinarily close to expressing with complete sincerity to his questioner. Yes, he had almost said, you are very nearly right; you are only just wrong. This unphrased response still echoed loud in his mind across what he could not help but see as the devastating chasm that this revelation and the impossibility of ever expressing it had cast between himself and the boy.

It was at the time when all of this was strongest within him that Leander had announced the imminent arrival of Maroo and had asked his friend to accompany him to the city Friday to see her. Steitler's first reaction had been one almost of horror, and he declined the invitation with a vehemence only faintly concealed. The thought of meeting Elizabeth once more now that he had come to recognize, by means of his encounter with Bone, the enmity she all too clearly bore him, was profoundly disconcerting. Nor would it, he had thought, for the same reason and also for that of an earlier indiscretion, be any less difficult to greet Elizabeth's mother, Maroo, the old lady who had not been pleased to answer what she had apparently looked upon as the unjustified impertinence of his letter to her. Furthermore, both of these interviews would doubtlessly take place before Leander, and that meant risking exposure in his eyes. Consequently, the reply he made to his young friend's invitation had been a firm and significant no.

What had come to appear the childishness and obscurity of avoiding the situation, the meeting with Elizabeth and Maroo, began to strike him as a more serious error than would be involved in merely going to the city as Lee had suggested, facing out whatever might have to be faced there, and risking whatever unpleasantness such an action might possibly entail. Unpleasant as it might be to see Elizabeth once more, to see her mother, whatever her attitude towards the indiscretion of his letter, could be nothing less than fascinating, and very probably delightful. As for Lee, Elizabeth would be, after all, even more anxious than he, Steitler, to keep from her son the truth of her relationship with his friend, and the niceness and ease of the meeting would unquestionably be maintained. In short, he decided, it would be easier to go than not to go. And it would be infinitely more interesting.

So it was that at mid-morning on Friday, the day following Simon's death, the young instructor and Leander Poor presented themselves at the door to Elizabeth's house. Neither of them had yet learned of Maroo's illness, but they were shortly enlightened by the trained nurse in white who admitted them. Mrs. Caven, they were told, had what might or might not be more than a very severe chest-cold. Her fever was high. The doctor was with her now as was Mrs. Poor, and would Mr. Poor and his friend be kind enough to wait in the living-room. A Mr. Motley was also there. If they had already met, would they excuse her so that she might return to the sick-room.

In face of these unexpected announcements, delivered so rapidly and with such an air of finality that there was no time for reply or further questioning, the young instructor, with a slow half-smile, his eyebrows slightly raised, turned towards Lee for whatever clarification or sympathetic acknowledgement the boy might verbally or merely with his expression, have to offer. But Lee offered nothing. For the hundredth time, though never perhaps so vividly, Steitler realized, as he followed him into the living-room, the completeness of their isolation one from another.

George Motley was discovered curled up at one end of a pale gray couch, one arm, the elbow deep in cushions, supporting his head, and the other holding erect the book which he seemed with profound interest to be reading. He appeared not to notice the two young men who had entered, but only wrinkled his brow fiercely as though some disturbing noise from the street or the sudden recognition of an incredible violation of good taste on the part, perhaps, of the author before him, had enforced his irritation. Not one of his thinning red hairs was out of place, and not even the quick wrinkles marred the shine of his freckled forehead. He was a portrait of well-groomed concentration as he continued to stare intently at his book. Lee was the first to address him.

At the sound of his voice the novelist wrenched himself from his reading and looked up in a splendor of surprise. In a moment he was on his feet and the book sprawled beside him on the carpet. How charming to see him again, he said as he shook the boy's hand warmly. And Mr. —?
The name had to be supplied him before he could complete his greeting to Steitler. He waved them into chairs and resumed his former seat on the couch.

"What's all this about Maroo?" asked Lee.

Motley's irrepressible gesture of delight at realizing his position of superior enlightenment was followed in an instant by a counter expression of the gravity which he was quick to recognize as required by such a position.

"She's not well, I'm afraid," he replied. "Not well at all." His implications were as sinister as he could manage with the room full of clear morning light and the candor of spring. It was difficult in such surroundings to think of sickness at all let alone any so probably fatal as he implied the old lady's to be.

"Is she conscious?" asked Steitler.

"Yes, does she know people and all that?" added Leander.

"Oh yes . . ." Motley was forced to explain that the old lady was quite herself in spite of her fever and the deep, sometimes uncontrollable cough. The doctor, he continued, had seemed rather more unwilling than unable to commit himself to a more specific diagnosis and would only say that it was too early yet to be certain. He was with her now, however, and more might soon be known. The novelist looked neither at Lee nor at Steitler as he spoke, but at the window before him. During the silence that followed his remarks, and as though to confirm them, could be heard the low, indecipherable tattoo of voices from a room far down the hall.

". . . and so there's nothing to do but wait." Motley finally concluded. Though it seemed to him evidence of the effectiveness of his implications and, therefore, like laughter following a jest, to be permitted almost as long as possible, the renewed silence grew, in truth, rather from Steitler's disapproval of what seemed to him the indelicacy not only of the older man's words but of his own unwarranted intrusion upon the situation with which they dealt, and from Leander's indifference to all but further, more definite information concerning that situation. Making the most of what he himself was nevertheless pleased to imagine his triumph, Motley walked quietly to the window, where he stood looking out into the morning and enjoying on the back of his small neck the wondering gaze of eyes that were actually otherwise occupied; eyes which, in their misunderstood reticence, saw not the back of the novelist figured against the paned daylight, but simply the daylight itself sprawled loosely among the softness and pastels of the living-room, and then, in a few moments, the sudden, almost imperceptible arrival there of Tristram Bone.

In flannel of the palest gray of doves he stood, immense, yet rather as a mist or cloud, it seemed, than as a living form made fast by a friend's illness and the morning light. So instantaneously had he entered not only the room but the already established situation, or so completely removed from them both did he seem despite his entrance to be, that the words with which they variously greeted him sounded as superfluous and awkward as though addressed to someone who had been sitting silently with them the entire time, either asleep or awake. Furthermore, these words, and the gestures by which they were accompanied, might well have been construed by any observer unacquainted with the language being used as meaning not so much "here is Tristram" as, rather, for such was his appearance, "where is he"—where behind the misted vestments of gray, white linen, daylight, is the living presence of the figure so recently arrived?

Motley had turned from the window, Steitler and Lee had arisen, and each faced him from different parts of the room, held him at bay among them, with this question invisibly pennanted through the soft and fragrant air they breathed. It was as if either they and the room were part of reality, or else he was, but not both.

Tristram, for that matter, had entered with a question of his own, a safer one than theirs, one that he could momentarily hide behind, and he asked it now, his expression betraying an utter lack of concern for whatever answer it might elicit.

"How is Maroo?" He did not hear Motley's reply, similar in purpose and implication to the one concluded a few moments before his arrival, but simply looked at the speaker and the young listeners unseeingly. Some words of Emma's turned slowly as though in crystal through his mind, and he counted them, scanned them, and pondered their meaning. "Everything now will be different," she had said.

The morning had come suddenly upon him, yet gently, as he looked back upon it, like a girl. It was spring, and soon it would be perhaps summer. There had been children playing in the streets as he passed by, or the streets had been empty, but a sweet, light wind had blown, and he had seen leaves almost transparent and curled like bits of chipped beef on the portable city trees. There had been somewhere, of course, an organ-grinder, he remembered; there had been somewhere an organ-grinder, of course, playing a tune for any penny, any tune for many who didn't care which tune. He remembered. The organ-grinder had had an organ, but he had had nothing else. The organ-grinder and his organ. But nothing, no, never, nothing else. Gracious and merciful Father, God of us all, he thought.

". . . and so there's nothing to do but wait." Motley concluded.

"Everything now will be different," answered the fat man. Steitler nodded, catching Bone's eye for the first time.

"You're right," he said. It was not evident either to Lee or to Motley that the two had met before, though neither had made any attempt to conceal the fact. Steitler conveyed this with his glance to Bone, who understood. "Everything has to be different every time something like this happens," continued the young instructor.

"It seems to me you're making an awful fuss about it," said Lee. "After all, for all we know it's no more than a rotten cold."

"Do you *try* to misunderstand, my friend," replied the young instructor almost sharply. Bone gave a faint smile to make what he was about to ask seem a silly, gay question, for he awaited the answer with desperation.

"How *is* she?" he asked.

"Who?" Motley spoke irritably, disagreeably unwilling to believe that Bone had not been listening to him.

"As Mr. Motley said," interposed Steitler, "we've no way of telling really. It's just a matter of waiting."

The novelist turned back to the window, clasping his hands behind him. Bone sank down on the couch, picked up a crystal cigarette cup in the shape of an opera hat and turned it slowly in his hands.

"I still think you're all making too much of a fuss," said Lee. Motley grunted without turning again from the window.

"It's a lovely, lovely morning." Bone leaned his head back against the couch as he spoke so that the sun fell full on his face.

"Maybe, under the circumstances, it would be better if we . . ." Steitler was not permitted to finish since down the hall a door opened, and in a moment the nurse appeared before them.

"Mrs. Caven wants to see you three," she announced, excluding Motley with her gesture, "and Doctor thinks it would be better if you all came together rather than one by one which would take too long and be too much. Mrs. Poor says would you wait, Mr. Motley."

Motley would, as it happened, and settled down again with his book as the others followed the nurse out.

Tristram, slightly in advance of the others, was the first to see Elizabeth, who stepped out of her mother's room, closed the door behind her, and leaned for a moment against it with her hand still on the knob. She looked unusually pale to him in the light brown dress she wore, and he reached out to take her hand in his, withdrawing it only when he saw that she had not noticed his gesture. Instead, it was her son she saw between himself and Steitler, and her son to whom she went first, embracing him, pressing his blond head down to her shoulder. Only then, as she kissed the boy's neck lightly, and even as she was engaged in this, did her eyes meet Bone's. There was neither forgiveness, nor the continuation of her anger at him, nor even any apparent recollection of that anger, in her look; she did not smile as often before at the sight of his heavy concern, and she did not weep as when last they had met at the time of Maroo's arrival. Her only expression seemed one of wonder at the fact alone of other figures there about her in the hallway. Bone looked away, then back in an instant to see her with triumphing grace and a similar absence of perceptible emotion shake Steitler's hand and then turn to him for his. With words meant largely, he guessed, for Leander's ears, yet as if, too, for her own reassurance, she thanked them both for their kindness in coming. Then, in another instant, in another voice, and with a new if still vague awareness in her eyes, she spoke with what was to at least two of her listeners a certain ambiguity.

"This is the last time you will see her, you know." She paused as though listening to her own words, glanced about her as though listening for an answer from one of them. "She wanted to see you. Is George all right? She's completely herself, but can't speak very well. She's terribly weak." She started to open the door. "Be as good as you can." Her words went out to each of them as she turned once more, and opened the door. The doctor nodded to her silently and passed by into the hall as they entered.

They had expected to see Maroo and a room rich with her presence and little else, but if the old lady was indeed the richest treasure there, she was only the more wisely safeguarded by the plethora of lesser wealth. Morning sunlight in long horizontals through the latticed blinds serenely puzzled the wide room by singling here and there disconnected shapes of brightness for predominance. One spray of a sea-green glass vaseful of lilacs caught the light and, like a wing, dipped through the shadow; a tall silver lamp reflected the motionless figure of Bone, whose fingers lulled the high-light on a polished chair-back; four bands of sun sufficed to identify the blue-and-silvered portrait of a girl as Elizabeth. On a low footstool knitting needles gleamed among gray skeins of wool. The only living thing so ennobled by the broken day was Leander, whose head of bright hair took like a golden casque the spring sun.

The bed, in contrast, projected in shadow from the far wall of the room away from the windows with no more than an indistinct geometry of light about its foot. Her head and shoulders propped slightly with pillows, Maroo lay there, her hands still on the white blanket at her sides, her hair no longer combed into a bun but curled in a loose braid against the fresh linen behind her. Except for a complete immobility, there was no look of illness about her; there was no odor of medicine, no bottle-littered table to mar the placidity with which, once seen, she made the room her own. Her eyes were open and had watched the entrance of her daughter and the three men who stood before her now as though in separate worlds and, altogether, in another world from hers, to wonder at her smile as Elizabeth presented to her the only stranger there. As if to save her breath she no more than whispered his name, Paul Steitler, as he approached to lift her hand from where it lay beside her, relinquishing it then to Tristram Bone who put it for an instant to his lips. Leander bent down clumsily and kissed her brow.

What the old lady saw was not what the others saw, and what she heard was something more or less than they, for above what seemed to her the low rushing of an unseen wind she heard fragments only of what they said; and through the dimness of the bedroom cut with strips of morning light through slatted blinds she saw no more than metamorphoses of fluttering figures, disparate shapes in flight through criss-crossed shadow; and yet she was, as had been said, herself. She was quite herself, as Motley had been forced to admit, with the difference only that she found herself obliged to deal with things that did not seem themselves to her. The change seemed theirs and not her own.

Only her grandson, who stood nearest her, his brown tweed jacket and red tie the only surfaces of plausibility and warmth, appeared to her a living unit. He was hers, she thought. If he were anyone's, he was then hers; or, more accurately, she thought, he was what he was, he was himself, because of her. Nor was he aware of this, which was as she had wanted it. So successfully had her hopes for him been realized, she understood, that he was invulnerable not only as far as the subtle perils of being alive were concerned, perils of which she had written him with quaint indirection in her letters, but as far as the source of his invulnerability, as far as herself, was concerned too. She had had only to watch him cross the room and to feel his kiss cool upon her forehead to be confident of this. Why, then, she wildly wondered, this instant of regret she felt, this nearness to tears, warm as a fever in her eyes, as he had turned from his embrace? Because— she knew and thrust from her as best she could her answer —because she had for a moment wanted, more than her life, some sign from him that he, at least, had understood; that he, if no one else, acknowledged there her gift to him. Yet in her deeper heart she was thankful that he gave no such sign, for what is expressed, she knew, ceases somehow to be, and should the boy acknowledge her gift, he would thereby lose it; should he say "Because of this old lady I am in some way safe now" he would be no longer safe. Yet might he only give some trivial, unconscious sign . . . She could speak, but not easily, her deep voice husky and faint with cold.

"Sit here, boy." Leander took the chair beside her bed. A face floating close above her in a patch of sun, drawn and heavy-eyed, the lips moist and glistening, rounded and great like a child's toy, revealed itself as Tristram's.

"Dear Maroo, I regret more than I'm at liberty just now to say that we could not have our dinner together last night."

"You look so tired, lad." The face seemed to grow larger as he bent to hear. "Tired," she repeated.

As he spoke again the rustling in her ears obliterated some of what he said, and she smiled at her own incongruous disability. He returned her smile, but persisted in his words, in an undertone, for her alone, his back to the others. She had missed a great deal already.

". . . only the hat, the hat left, and no little head nor anything, you see. Tell me, what is there for me now since you, if any, forgive me, know, can tell me such a thing. Can you? I must not trouble you, but—this has happened. It's not his life I mourn, you know—I do not mourn—but mine, costly and fading, fading. Oh, if any, you will, do you, know?"

"Know . . ." she echoed his word uncertainly.

"You say 'no'? 'No'? Then who?" He drew back, and his face was lost for her in shadow; only something gold about his vest flickered like a question.

"Tristram."

The old lady felt a hand cool on her forehead as Elizabeth spoke.

"Don't try to talk, dear. You mustn't tire yourself for all our sakes. We'll do the talking. You mustn't tire yourself."

"Nonsense," Maroo said, controlling her cough so that she could continue. "The old citizen's got herself an audience, and she's going to make the best of it while she's able. What time is it?"

"Almost eleven, Mrs. Caven." A young man's hand held a watch before her. The crystal cast its reflection on the ceiling.

"Paul Steitler, mother."

"I know. Leander's friend."

"A friend of the family's by now," Lee said with a little laugh. "He'll worm his way anywhere, that one. Watch him like a hawk."

There was a brief silence during which Maroo caught Steitler's profile as he turned towards her grandson. His eyes were wide and luminous beneath thick brows; no detailed texture of his skin, lips, hair escaped her. His teeth showed wet and white as he laughed, and then he looked for the first time directly at her.

"What an exquisite lack of tact your grandson has."

She did not answer him but asked instead,

"What is the matter with Tristram? He was trying to tell me something just now."

"*You* speak of tact!" said Elizabeth to the young instructor with a smile that was understood differently by each who observed it.

"Watch him like a hawk!" Leander laughed again.

"He is looking out of your window as though nothing were the matter at all, Mrs. Caven. Are we tiring you?"

"Like a hawk!"

"He was trying to tell me something just now."

"What was he trying to tell you, dear?"

"He's an evil lad, my Leander, not answering his old ancestor's letters, but I'll forgive him by and by."

"Gosh, Maroo. Sit here, Mr. Bone." The boy stood up as Tristram approached.

"It's a beautiful, beautiful morning, Maroo. Perhaps nothing is different after all. Perhaps she was wrong."

"By and by. I'll forgive him by and by. What's that?"

"Who is that knocking?" Elizabeth faded towards the door.

"Just little George Motley," whispered the novelist standing on the threshold. "I really must leave, Elizabeth. A luncheon engagement with a fool. You will forgive me? Is there anything I can do?" He spoke rapidly in a whisper scarcely audible to the others.

"No, George. Nothing. Thank you. I'm sorry; forgive *me*."

"Well, then. Oh, Maroo!" he called out towards the bed and the figures standing near the bed.

"Bon voyage, dear Maroo! Bon voyage!" His voice trailed off into a stately silence broken only by the clicking of the door as he closed it behind him. The old lady's eyes brightened questioningly through the shadow.

"I want more light, Elizabeth. Light!" She started to cough.

"Yes, yes," her daughter answered. "Tristram, the blind! Don't try to talk, mother. The blind! We must all go now. Where is the nurse!"

With a movement of great force, Tristram tore open the blind covering the large window opposite the bed. The room was confounded with sunlight.

Overwhelmed with the sudden brilliance, Maroo was aware at first of no more than a spinning, wheeling brightness and the fluttering of figures as they shifted and gave way about her through the vast illuminations and the freshness of day. Her head sank more deeply into the pillows while the rushing noise as of wind or many wings grew stronger, pierced here and there by wordless exclamations, murmurs and cries, lonely and keen like the cries of birds.

Of the four who had stood at her side, three now were gone, or almost gone, flown up and off it seemed, yet circling still, wings spread, around, around, through what appeared a sky high, high and blue above.

And one remained. For an instant she saw him, Leander,

unchanged and unchanging, unmoved, there beside her. If the three birds winged wild above him too, he neither saw nor heard them. For all the circling, dappled brilliance, tall and motionless he stood fast in the morning sun. She reached out to touch him but could not. The glitter of her ancient eyes was lost in the devastation of light.

Meridian Fiction

12 East 22 Street, New York 10, New York

All Meridian Fiction publications are contemporary works of literary distinction deserving the broader readership made possible by paperback editions. They are printed on specially made Meridian Eggshell paper and Perfect Bound for durability.
MERIDIAN FICTION IS DISTRIBUTED BY MERIDIAN BOOKS, INC.

MERIDIAN BOOKS

12 East 22 Street, New York 10, New York

Titles listed here are not necessarily available in the British Empire

THE MERIDIAN

Twice yearly, in the spring and fall publishing seasons, Meridian Books take to newspaper format and issue *The Meridian,* a lively eight-page tabloid distributed free to thousands of subscribers. Its purpose, like that of any good house organ, is to acquaint readers with the present and future activities of the various imprints of the firm: Meridian Books, Meridian Giants, Living Age Books, Greenwich Editions, the Jewish Publication Society Series, Meridian Fiction, and Meridian Periodicals. The news is scattered in pre-publication reviews, selections from forthcoming books, guest features by authors, blurbs on projects vague and concrete—even in pictures. Among the standard features are the ever-popular "Tax Tips for the Teacher" and a complete list of all titles published by Meridian Books. For a free, unlimited subscription, write to:

The Meridian
12 East 22 Street
New York 10, New York

MERIDIAN BOOKS

12 East 22 Street, New York 10, New York

MERIDIAN GIANTS

MG1   MYSTICISM *by Evelyn Underhill*
MG2   MEDIEVAL PANORAMA *by G. G. Coulton*
MG3   PROLEGOMENA TO THE STUDY OF GREEK RELIGION *by Jane Harrison*
MG4   MY LIFE IN ART *by Constantin Stanislavski*
MG5   THE ROMANTIC AGONY *by Mario Praz*
MG6   PHILOSOPHIES OF INDIA *by Heinrich Zimmer*
MG7   PLATO: THE MAN AND HIS WORK *by A. E. Taylor*
MG8   FRANCE AGAINST HERSELF *by Herbert Luethy*
MG9   THE LITERATURE OF THE SPANISH PEOPLE *by Gerald Brenan*
MG10   FILM FORM *and* THE FILM SENSE *by Sergei Eisenstein*
MG11   LITERATURE IN AMERICA *edited by Philip Rahv*
MG12   THE DISSOCIATION OF A PERSONALITY *by Morton Prince*
MG13   A TREASURY OF YIDDISH STORIES *edited by Irving Howe and Eliezer Greenberg*
MG14   CHINESE CIVILIZATION *by Marcel Granet*
MG15   THE ORIGINS OF TOTALITARIANISM *by Hannah Arendt*
MG16   THE PHILOSOPHY OF SPINOZA *by Harry Austryn Wolfson*
MG17   THE MAN OF THE RENAISSANCE *by Ralph Roeder*
MG18   NEW YORK PLACES & PLEASURES *by Kate Simon*
MG19   THE PLACE OF VALUE IN A WORLD OF FACTS *by Wolfgang Köhler*
MG20   FROM THE N.R.F. *edited by Justin O'Brien*
MG21   JAIL KEYS MADE HERE AND OTHER SIGNS *photographs by Lee Boltin*

MERIDIAN LIBRARY

ML1   ROMAN SOCIETY FROM NERO TO MARCUS AURELIUS *by Samuel Dill*
ML2   A DICTIONARY OF CLASSICAL ANTIQUITIES *by Oskar Seyffert*
ML3   AN INTRODUCTION TO THE LITERATURE OF THE OLD TESTAMENT *by S. R. Driver*
ML4   THE RELIGION OF THE SEMITES *by W. Robertson Smith*
ML5   EARLY GREEK PHILOSOPHY *by John Burnet*
ML6   PROLEGOMENA TO THE HISTORY OF ANCIENT ISRAEL *by Julius Wellhausen*
ML7   THE GRAMMAR OF SCIENCE *by Karl Pearson*
ML8   A HISTORY OF AESTHETIC *by Bernard Bosanquet*
ML9   AN ENCYCLOPEDIA OF RELIGION AND RELIGIONS *by E. Royston Pike*
ML10   ROMAN SOCIETY IN THE LAST CENTURY OF THE WESTERN EMPIRE *by Samuel Dill*

LIVING AGE BOOKS

published by MERIDIAN BOOKS, INC.

12 East 22 Street, New York 10, New York

Titles listed here are not necessarily available in the British Empire

EXISTENTIALISM FROM DOSTOEVSKY TO SARTRE

Edited, selected, and introduced by Walter Kaufmann

What is existentialism? It is perhaps the most misunderstood of modern philosophic positions—misunderstood by reason of its broad popularity and general unfamiliarity with its origins, representatives, and principles. Walter Kaufmann, author of *Nietzsche* (Meridian Books, M25), is eminently qualified to present and interpret the insights of existentialism as they occur and are deepened by the major thinkers who express them. There are extensive selections from the writings of Sartre ("The Wall," "Existentialism," and the chapter on "Self-Deception" from *Being and Nothingness*); two lectures from Karl Jaspers's work *Reason and Existenz;* original translations of "On My Philosophy," by Jaspers and "The Way Back into the Ground of Metaphysics," by Heidegger; and material from Dostoevsky, Kierkegaard, Nietzsche, Rilke, and Camus.

M39   *322 pages*

". . . a first-rate introduction to existentialism."

The Review of Metaphysics

". . . it is an admirable introduction to a state of mind and heart we must all attempt to understand."

CRANE BRINTON, *The American Scholar*

FREUD AND THE TWENTIETH CENTURY

Edited by Benjamin Nelson

The twentieth century is now being called "the Freudian century" and "the age of the Freudian revolution." For a single man to dominate a century his work must affect all manner of thought and human activity. Reinhold Niebuhr, Jacques Maritain, Abram Kardiner, Alfred Kazin, Will Herberg, E. H. Gombrich, and many others examine the impact of Freud upon literature, the arts, religion, philosophy, psychiatry—the whole of culture and history.   M45   *314 pages*

". . . an excellent picture of the influence of Freud and the position of Freudian science in the twentieth century. It is to be recommended to any student. . . ."
                                              Psychiatric Quarterly

THE VARIETIES OF HISTORY
From Voltaire to the Present

Edited, selected, and introduced by Fritz Stern

The greatest of historians, from the time of Voltaire, approach the records of the past with definite convictions about their meaning and implication. As their sense of what is important in history differed, so the kinds of history they wrote differed. Represented in this volume, among other historians, are Ranke, Michelet, Marx, Mommsen, Bury, Trevelyan, Beard, Meinecke, and Namier. Almost half the volume, including a long essay by Johan Huizinga, has been translated for the first time.   M37   *427 pages*

"With a masterly essay, Professor Stern introduces selections from great and other historians of modern times on the meaning and purposes of history. His book ought to be in the hands of all graduate students and many of their teachers."

    BOYD C. SHAFER, *The American Historical Review*

". . . the best collection of its sort I have seen, and he [Professor Stern] is an excellent guide."

    GEOFFREY BARRACLOUGH, *The Nation*

NEW POETS OF ENGLAND AND AMERICA

Edited and selected by Donald Hall, Robert Pack, and Louis Simpson

This volume offers (in many cases for the first time) a representative selection from the poetry of fifty-two younger American and English poets. As Robert Frost observed in his introduction, "all poets I have ever heard of struck their note long before forty. . . . The statistics are all in favor of their being as good and lyric as they will ever be. . . . The poets of this group . . . need live to write no better, need only wait to be better known for what they have written."

M50   *351 pages*

". . . to see so much liveliness and accomplishment should stir our imagination and our hope."

LOUISE BOGAN, *The New Yorker*

"To bring 36 new American poets together with 16 new English poets was a daring and useful venture. It is a solid confirmation of a very important fact: The cause, the art, the practice of poetry are flourishing still. . . . This book is a strength to all who want confirmation that a depth of literary culture exists today. . . ."

PAUL ENGLE, *New York Post*